T0162694

Catscratch Fever
and Other Stories

From the Journals of Skinny Malink

Katherine Baccaro

iUniverse, Inc.
New York   Bloomington

Catscratch Fever and Other Stories
From the Journals of Skinny Malink

iUniverse books may be ordered through booksellers or by contacting:

iUniverse
1663 Liberty Drive
Bloomington, IN 47403
www.iuniverse.com
1-800-Authors (1-800-288-4677)

ISBN: 978-1-4401-6005-9 (sc)
ISBN: 978-1-4401-6004-2 (dj)
ISBN: 978-1-4401-6006-6 (ebk)

Printed in the United States of America

iUniverse rev. date: 8/18/2009

IN MEMORY OF JEZEBEL
WHO DANCED THE SHRIMP DANCE
AND SANG THE SHRIMP SONG

BANANA BABY

Imelda Pogue, the village witch, burst into Joe's Java Nut Joint when the morning crowd was gathered for their communal grunts and very early coffee fixes. Imelda is so eerie, bombastic too. Sometimes it's an embarrassment to be recognized by her. But she saw me and she pointed at me with her long and crooked finger. "Oh, *here* you are at last!" she shouted, her bony digit aimed right at me. It all seemed positively accusatory. The town is very indulgent about her, but me, I can be a little bit afraid.

Imelda is a human anomaly. She really looks exceedingly peculiar. This morning she looked like hell, if you really want to know. I swear her skin is vaguely green. I suspect she doesn't wash too much. People say that she has a big heart. Her torso is big enough, maybe, to accommodate her huge engine but, by that measure, one must consider the capacity of a small head. I never saw an adult with such a tiny cranium. She appeared in the coffee shop that morning with her large body swathed in a voluminous great coat of military khaki while on her pin head sat a big blue cowboy hat. Electric blue. Her red hair sticking out all around from under it signaled distress. The overall impression was furious and desperate.

"I thought I'd find someone I knew in there," she said. That came as a shock since I really did not know her, didn't much want to. "I need you to be witness to an act of unspeakable cruelty," she screamed. Everyone was looking at us. With Imelda glaring at me and all eyes upon me I had to feel guilty. No idea why. Or maybe I felt guilty because a strong desire to kick her right out the door was arising in my breast. My morning cappuccino lay smoldering in front of me. It looked as if I wasn't going to get to savor it this morning. Imelda was scaring me. It was said of her that she could deliver curses. Naturally with the rest of civilized society I have no belief in such nonsense but it's never wise to tempt the devil. Before I could say a word she grabbed my arm and pulled me toward the door. She physically pulled me out behind the shop and toward the garbage bins. I followed meekly.

"Listen!" she commanded. I tried being reasonable and polite. I thought I had a madwoman to humor, but I was getting more scared by the minute. Close up she was terrifying. I truly thought she might be dangerous. As she commanded, I stood there listening to the garbage.

I heard nothing. I shook my head.

"Listen harder," Imelda insisted. Her fingernails were digging into my arm. Her face was contorted with something, maybe rage, maybe the effort of concentrated listening.

And then I heard it too. The song of the garbage can.

Squeaks.

" Shame! Shame!" she cried to me and to the skies. "A disgrace on the human race. That's what it is."

"What is?"

To my consternation she appeared to dive into the garbage pail, still fulminating, her words still pouring forth, now almost undecipherable. She heaved up seconds later with something she'd plucked from the bins -- garbage. On a crumpled newspaper page lay a tiny being, squeaking full force. She thrust it under my nose. "See this!" she shouted. "A living thing. Disposed of thus by stupid barbarians!"

The vehement way she spouted the words sounded like an accusation. I tried to maintain my calm. "Imelda, I promise you. I didn't put it there."

"Perhaps not, but you're Joe's friend and this is his garbage can. I want you to go back in the Joint and tell every one what we found out here."

"There's nothing Joe can do about what strangers pop into his garbage can."

"Somebody should be able to do something," she continued but now her attention was diverted by the squeaker in her hand. "This guy wants to live," she remarked. "He's actually trying to spit at me!"

"What will you do with it? Will you keep it?"

"I can't," she grunted. "In this cycle I'm commanded to do dogs."

That didn't make too much sense. Under the circumstances I didn't expect too much sense.

"A kitten this young requires constant care," she declared. "There's a German woman in town that cares for wildlife. I will appeal to her. Maybe she'll take it. Maybe she knows somebody who will," Imelda declared, and furiously stomped away muttering things, probably curses and incantations, still growling her righteous indignation. I could see her high green boots punishing the ground at every step. She walked like a Nazi SS officer.

A crazy women. Scouting garbage pails.

I leaned over the edge of the receptacle. Stuff in there: boxes, wrappers, banana peels, spaghetti, coffee grounds, and sauce, lots of sauce.

One of the banana peels was moving!

I plucked that wretched piece of existence out of the dross with a bread wrapper. I guessed it must be a kitten though it certainly didn't look like one. "Imelda!" I cried. But it was no use. Imelda was gone. Her retreating form had evaporated in the distance.

The banana peel lay inert. I knew I had seen it move. Now I blinked. I saw a tiny body, its shape rising and falling with shallow breathing. I could see its little heart beating. So what does one do with a piece of life emerging from stinking banana peels? Every time it moved my insides moved with it. I never had such a reaction before. There was life manifesting itself out of a pile of dregs and right on a piece of waxy paper in the palm of my trembling hand.

It lived. Something must be done. I immediately took my burden to The Petseteria, our town's veterinary establishment. This was my first meeting with the eminent Dr. Woo, which ultimately developed into a lengthy and incredibly expensive acquaintance. I entered his office in a state of hysteria, thinking the creature might die at any moment. All this while, even though I was shaking very hard, I held the small bundle steadily balanced on the palm of my hand.

"Be cool. It's a kitten,' he said because I didn't actually know. "A little male. We'll put it away for you."

"Put it away? What's that supposed to mean? Aren't you going to help it to live?"

"No way, Jose. Do you have any idea how difficult it is to care for an animal this young? The time? The cost? It's like an infant. It may even crop up with birth defects. This one, for example, looks stunted.

"Often with these abandoned infants there is insufficient development of the cerebellum. The mother herself would throw him out. Besides, it's been lying in garbage. Germs. Corruption. It has endured enough, I assure you. It can only be a mercy to send it on to where it's bound to go anyway."

But I couldn't. I saw this dirty little thing striving for breath. I could see its heart beating. *Imelda Pogue hexed me,* I thought. *She wished a curse on me.*

Dr. Woo thought this was funny. He can be an exceptionally droll man in moments of dire distress. I guess he thinks it helps. After patiently explaining the care and feeding of such a kitten and, at exorbitant cost to me, he provided the tiny doll-size bottle and the powder to make the thin formula required. "Good luck with the banana baby, Ms Skinny Malinck," he said. "You know the old saying about beating a dead horse? Well, you're loving a dead cat."

But he wasn't dead. He had moved. I saw him move.

That's when my adventure began. I had to prepare the formula. Nothing seemed to happen when I placed the nipple to the kitten's mouth. I sprawled on the couch and put the kitten on my lap. It stirred. Suddenly it began to suck, or try to. The sensation that awoke inside me was overwhelming. I glowed. In that moment I felt everything – love and pride and the enormous joy of maternity. The little kitten suckled. He wanted to eat. He wanted to live. A miracle.

And he stank. I took a rough cloth and with warm water began to stroke him very gently across the head and back. He squeaked. I didn't want to hurt him but it had to be done. He was filthy. The stroking seemed to be achieving something. A color change was taking place. I washed the little paws, marveling at the tiny pink pads, small and tender as a baby's buttons. The compact face, eyes squinched closed. He was so pretty. He was coming up white, pure white now. White as snow, a snow flake. A snowflake with nose as pink as the paw buds. The delicate translucent little ears. Oh, he was so pretty! I loved him.

Most gently I turned him over. The little belly, fuller after the few drops he'd swallowed. The tiny anus, like a small pink rosebud, suddenly emitted a minute benefice – so stinky I almost fainted. Now I really was his joyous mama, reveling in his odiferous life, a gift from the witch woman, Imelda Pogue.

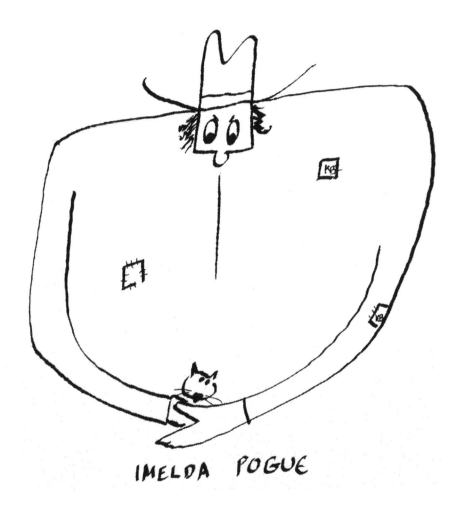

IMELDA POGUE

DR. W.

Since he had first given evidence of life in the palm of my hand, Snowflake thrived in health and beauty. He was handsome. He was of a noble bearing, regal in his movements. He was impeccable in his toilette, constantly washing himself until he sparkled like a real snowflake. And he was a gourmet, enjoying the gamier pates of meat and fish, even odiferous cheeses. He had a strange reaction to bananas. He went slightly berserk when banana peels were in our garbage pail. In spite of his miraculous refuse-bin origin, in time he became an elegant cat, yet he differed from ordinary cats in several ways. In the first place I, who had abhorred cats, now loved him. In no time I found he was firmly entrenched in my heart.

There were problems. Apparently Dr. Woo's prediction of damage to the cerebellum had some validity. There were things missing in Snowflake. First of all, in spite of having the appetite of a Bengal tiger, he didn't grow. He started as very small kitten and small he remained right into adulthood, so small that I could call him "my mini-cat." Another difference not at first apparent, Snowflake was deaf. Because he was so clever I did not immediately perceive the symptoms. He always stayed near me. When awake, he always fixed his eyes on me. And he would stare. They were enormous, luminous eyes, possibly seeming larger because he was so small. He knew how to use those orbs. He would fix me in the power of his green eyes.

I was the source of all things good in his cat-life so he stayed near and watched my every move. From my motions he could deduct the next feature in his daily routine – feed the cat, brush the cat, sleep with the cat (my body a warm place to create a nestling place for the cat), provide treats for the cat, dangle a string to play with the cat. Any motions not directly benefiting the cat, Snowflake ignored.

As far as intelligence went, Snowflake demonstrated his superior intellect by learning to tell time. How many cats can do that? Five o'clock is when the dinner dish went down and five o'clock is when he appeared by his spot in the kitchen. Seasonal variations in the light made no difference. Snowflake could tell time. He always knew when it was five o'clock.

While coping with the realization of Snowflake's anomalies I naturally got to know Dr. Woo very well. Dr. Leopold Woo was a good vet but a rather more comedian than his worried and paying clients might desire. A small man with an oriental cast to his features.

Thick lenses magnified his constant twinkle. Dr. Woo thought he was funny. He clearly thought Snowflake's minuscule size was comical too. He called him "pygmy cat" or "banana boy" or "the teeny weeny." Snowflake didn't mind that at all. He purred like a diesel when Woo examined him. Snowflake loved the human touch. He easily went into a gentle roar. He purred for me and all my friends. He purred when he even looked at me. He purred when I spoke to him which, in my solitude, I did frequently. For a minicat Snowflake had an operatic purr box.

But he was deaf.

"Are you sure, Doctor?" I asked.

"Deaf. Definitely deaf. Def deaf, you might say." Dr. Woo suffered from bouts of antiquated slang.

"But. Doctor, he reacts when I speak to him."

"Sure. That's visual. He sees you," he said. He put my poor, defective kitten on the table. "Look in here," Woo instructed, indicating the cat's ears. "You see all those little hairs?"

"I do."

"And whiskers. Whiskers on his cheeks. Whiskers on his eyebrows. Whiskers everywhere. He's a regular forest of whiskers."

"And handsome they are, too," I said fondly. "Very elegant like the fountains of Versailles."

"More than elegant," Woo replied. "Very useful. Every one of those stiff hairs and whiskers is a little antenna, cocked to detect vibrations and changes in the wind."

"He can hear?"

"Not in the usual way," said Woo. "But well, perhaps, but well enough to defend himself from vacuum cleaners," Woo said and that was actually funny because, just that morning, Snowflake, who could leap many times the length of his small body, had jumped up to his penthouse on top of the china closet when I had begun to vacuum the floor.

"Then he's not handicapped?"

"But he really is. Maybe I'll get him little handicapped placard to hang off his tail." Woo said.

I never could tell how seriously to take the man. He delighted in being silly.

One memorable day he phoned me. "You with the banana cat," he began, "I have a favor to ask of you."

Almost any transaction with Dr. Woo came to cost a pretty penny so I was cautious. "I don't think Snowflake's in need of your good offices, Doctor, I won't have time to bring him in this week. Besides I can't afford your priceless treatments right now. I'm broke."

"Won't cost you a cent, Miss Skinny Malinck. No, no. No charge for this. No need to come in. The favor will come to you." He chuckled. "You can do this favor at your very own home.

"I have here right now a member of the scientific community, who would like to visit your cat."

"Snowflake? Why?"

"I'm sure you are aware, lady fair, that you have a very special cat. It is for that very specialness that this researcher would like to interview him."

I said nothing. Interview a cat? What nuttiness would Woo come up with next? But I agreed. My curiosity was aroused.

"Good," he said. "She will telephone you for an appointment. Her name is Dr. Alda Patalda."

MEOW IS MIOU

At an unholy hour of the next morning, without calling for an appointment, the scientific researcher appeared at my door. She was an appalling apparition. An enormous dome of hair topped her squat body. It was twice the size of her big head. This jet black cupola studded with stars and dime store gems distracted me from her terrifying countenance, but only for a moment. Her face was far too peculiar to go unnoticed. At a glance it seemed as if she had no face. A round dish. A horrifying surface which seemed flat, almost as if it was something painted on the collar of her dress. As visages go, I would call it daunting. She'd drawn, in greasy black, eyes, lips, even outlined the bridge of an impressive nose. She was so strange. I tried the impossible name. "Are you Alda Patalda?" I asked.

"I am DOCTOR Alda Patalda," she corrected as she swept into my living room. She was a short woman, sort of built like a mailbox, and her forward motion was chunky and awkward, as if she had just gotten off roller skates. She carried a silver case. "Where is the aberration?" she asked.

"Excuse me?"

"The midget cat."

The use of the word "aberration" to refer to my little darling quite put me off. There was an abruptness to her manner that didn't help at all. I gritted my teeth realizing I just had to get through this visit without committing murder.

"I came to see the deviant," Alda Patalda explained.

"Deviant" didn't sit any better with me than "aberration."

"You refer to my cat? He's a perfect cat," I said. "Perfect in every way." An unexpected maternal instinct rose up fiercely within me. I longed to kick Alda right in her patalda.

"Didn't Woo tell me there was a deaf cat here, a cat deaf from birth?"

"Snowflake is deaf, but not deviant."

As if I would deliver up my beautiful Snowflake to this rude woman! "Why?" I said. "What do you need to see him for?"

"I guess that idiot Woo didn't tell you," she said airily. "I am a doctor of linguistics … a very specialized branch of linguistics. Do you even know what philology is?" she inquired in a really snotty way.

"Enough to know there is no connection with my cat."

"Oh, but there is," insisted DOCTOR Alda Patalda. "You see I am the world's foremost authority on the language of the cat. I have been wanting to study the language of a cat that never heard its mother since it is to be assumed the earliest learning comes from the maternal font."

"That's ridiculous. A meow is a miou. And Snowflake has a mother. Me. I'm his mother."

"In your ignorance, you probably think so," she said. "There is a difference between meow and meeerhow, and there is even the low buzzing of mrrrr. Not to mention the regional forms and dialectal inflections. And the richness of insult. Nobody can make more denigrating remarks than a cat. They carry still other meanings. If you had ears to hear with you would be cognizant of all these variations, unless of course, your deaf kitty cannot make them."

What a crock! "Of course he can." I said. "He's a cat, really, truly a cat. He has always made the natural sounds."

"And what does he say when he is angry? I bet there are a lot of rrrwwws in it." Here the woman began to make series of cat calls. She was amazing, really. She had a mouthful of teeth and they came into play as she demonstrated the various cat-calls. "Cats are very resourceful and smart. They have expressions for almost everything, everything that really concerns them, that is."

I was more and more astonished.

"I am composing a dictionary of cat terms and their meanings in standard English though, of course, I speak Cat very fluently."

"I suppose I should make an attempt at it, then," I said, "Though you'll probably say I could never lose my strong American accent."

"Exactly!" agreed Doctor Alda Patalda. "But my brochure on the various sounds and their correct phonology would be of definite help to you. If you would only try." From her silver case she extracted a fat pamphlet. "FELINOGLOSSIA" it said on the cover. She thrust it at me.

At a glance I saw pages and pages of complex diacritical marks, the ones you are used to like long signs and schwas plus some symbols and numerical combinations that looked invented and absolutely imaginary.

"May I speak with your cat?"

"No," I replied. "In the interest of peaceful cohabitation, I never interrupt his meals or his naps."

"Oh, yes, of course," she said, as if she completely took my meaning which surprised me because I had no idea what I was talking about. "Well, perhaps you would like to study this compilation which, I assure you, will facilitate your comprehension and communication in Felinese."

She indicated the brochure still in my hand. "How much?" I asked.

"Five dollars," said DOCTOR Alda Patalda quickly.

The minute she left I called Dr. Woo. "Dr. Woo, I just got rid of that weird woman you sent me."

He was laughing so hard he could hardly answer me. "I thought you would enjoy her," he said. I'm sending her to all my clients that have 'special' cats, which is all the patients in the world who do have cats. Did you give her five bucks?"

"Yes," I said, "but only in the interest of peaceful cohabitation. Meow is still miou as far as I'm concerned."

THE CAT LOVERS' SOCIETY

Dr. Woo is a cut-up. At least he thinks he is. He sent DOCTOR Alda Patalda to a bunch of his cat clients and he also spread some words about my mini-cat, Snowflake. Sometimes he calls my kitten the "banana baby," sometimes the "garbage kitty." I find that a little offensive but Snowflake doesn't seem to mind. Snowflake actually likes Dr. Woo and I guess that says something about the man. I have always believed that animals can read into character and intention before humans can even begin to guess.

Not long after DOCTOR Alda Patalda's visit I had a phone call. "Hi," said a melodious voice. "Dr. Woo, your merry medical man, gave me your number. My name is Rosemary Fingerhat. I'm the president of the Ailurophilia Society."

"Ailurophilia? What's that? A disease?"

"No, just the love for cats. I want to talk to you about Alda Patalda, the cat philologist," said Rosemary Fingerhat.

"You mean DOCTOR Alda Patalda?"

"Well, maybe. Doctor of something. Some form of philology, as she claims."

"I think she just stuck the label onto her name to add dignity to a name that otherwise sounds rather ludicrous. Tell me what I can do for your ridiculous-sounding society, DOCTOR Rosemary Fingerhat."

She began laughing. "You're right," she admitted. "My name sounds pretty coocoo too, but there's not too much I can do about it. I considered changing it to Rosemary Thimble and that was just as silly. I guess I shall just have to wear it. Fingerhat it must remain since all my children are Fingerhats, But what about your name? Skinny Malinck! That's what I was told by the medical comedian. That sounds kind of frivolous to me."

"Is that what Woo told you? Oh, he's a funny, funny man. Never let him in on anything you don't want published. Sally Malinck is actually my name. Skinny is an old nickname, especially droll since I am hardly skinny anymore. I made a mistake telling that to Dr. Woo. But some of my very old friends still call me 'Skinny.'"

"I like 'Skinny Malinck.' It has a crispy sound to it, like breakfast cereal poured out of a new box. And it sounds like a friend of mine," said Rosemary, "which I hope you are going to be. Now tell me what you found out from our friend, DOCTOR Alda Patalda, the cat philologist," she requested in that musical voice of hers.

I brought out the brochure which I had left on the table. It was a serious looking little folder printed in a sort of mimeographed style. It looked like copy put out by school kids or little church clubs that have no money. Doric columns, obviously hand drawn, framed the pretentious cover. "FELINE GLOSSARY," it announced, "Compiled by Doctor Alda Patalda, DFF, PHC, Chairperson of the Department of Catology, Animal Communication Section, St. Kitkins University, Balboa, East Pacific Division." I read all this information to Rosemary Fingerhat.

"St. Kitkins? You think there could actually be such a place?"

"Anything is possible in a world where alda pataldas can march right up to your front door early in the morning. But wait a second," I said. "There's more. Right here it says, 'Studies toward a Definitive Comprehension of Auditory Cat Communications in the Twenty-first Century, Honorary awards conferred by the Feline Associates of Tabbyport, Maine, The Backalley Society of Calico, Florida, and the Pattypaw Alliance of Brooklyn, New York. European accolades to be described in the 2009 edition (under preparation) with additional testimonials by Drs. Cattiana Catlova, Leslie Meowiss, and the Most Honorable Kitty Alexander, ACA Emeritus.'"

"Holy ravioli!" exclaimed Rosemary Fingerhat. "You've got to give the woman credit for colossal nerve. What's inside this very pretentious brochure?"

"Not much information included. It is eight pages of diacritical marks, some of them familiar, some of them absolutely fantastic, science fiction signs, maybe. They wouldn't help me to pronounce BOO. Then there is a short list of words and phrases, most of them utilitarian, as far as cats are concerned, that is like, 'food, mouse, milk, leave me alone, curb the dog, shut up, go to hell.' And there are a few incomprehensible expressions included, for example: 'compound interest, prime rate, tax shelter, mortgage spread.' Whenever would a cat have the need to say such things?"

"Only a financial advisor cat when explaining the money crisis," said Rosemary Fingerhat, laughing. "Seriously though, Skinny Malinck, don't you think there was more to what the woman claimed than what the woman actually said?"

"About what?"

"About cats and their ways and methods of communication."

"Rosemary, you and I know they communicate. But it is more in the manner of body language than in discreet words. When Snowflake wants to be petted he knows how to make himself so seductive it is almost embarrassing. And he is always right near me to be sure his message hits the right person. When he can't get the message across he just stares and stares until I uncomfortably get the idea that something is amiss."

"And there are tones of voice," Rosemary added. "When my cats want a treat they let out the most pathetic series of whimpering cries. It's sort of 'I'm dy-y-y-ing!' Then, if I present them with something they don't like they just march off with their little pink noses in the air, dying no longer."

"Snowflake does that too."

"Your Snowflake is deaf, I'm told."

"Deaf and miniaturized, but very communicative."

"I want you to join the Ailurophile Society. That's why I'm calling. Please tell me you'll join. The only requirement is that you need to have a special cat."

"Snowflake is special all right."

"You'll never find a single cat owner in this town who won't tell you exactly the same thing. 'My cat is special.'" Rosemary assured me, laughing. "It's a <u>very</u> big club,"

"Are you going to try to unmask poor DOCTOR Alda Patalda?"

"Did you give her five dollars?"

"I did."

"So did thirteen others of the fifteen owners that Dr. Woo listed for her. That's forty-five bucks. Enough to eat for a while. After that she'll be coming to see me for the Ailurophile roster, I suppose."

"And you'll unmask her?"

"No. For what it's worth, I think I'll give her our whole list. Some of those tightwads won't part with a fart much less release a nickel. Let her gather as much as she can. After all, people can always say no, and Dr. Woo told me that she is penniless, just living on her nerve and fanciful wits. You know, when all's said and done, Woozy is really a good guy."

"I know," I agreed, "because Snowflake told me so."

THE AILUROPHILIA SOCIETY

At Rosemary Fingerhat's behest I became a member of the Ailurophilia Society. At first I did not realize the size of the organization. After a while I began to understand that it was gigantic, an informal collection of extremely diverse individuals, so many that they could have marched together and overthrown the government of a mid-sized nation. And they might have done so too, had it been in the interests of international catdom. Of course, a large enrollment was to be expected since the only requirement was that the individual member must have a special cat, a cat out of the ordinary in some way. Every cat owner in our town and probably in the world had such a creature. It's the nature of the beast.

There was fierce partisanship among some of the members. The Siamese, whose ancient lineage and royal characteristics were fiercely defended by their owners, might be scorned and denigrated by the Abyssinians and their owners. But clearly the owners of the Alley cats could put them all away.

No one could be more Alley than my Snowflake. He continued to amaze me. He was no larger than a kitten but daily demonstrated that he had a fully developed brain. Deafness did not impede his powers of communication which he expressed in song and even in dance. His song would be delivered in a high soprano with short notes, or with tweetings like the birds in the trees, which the poor kitty did not imitate. He could never hear them. At times he emitted a flat and raspy sound to express degrees of disappointment or personal disapproval. When I would walk by without acknowledging him he gave out something very like a musical burp, guaranteed to startle me into attention. It was his way of saying, "I'm here."

The incredible thing was that, though he could not hear, he knew I could and so he continued to use sound for me.

There was also a song of anger. I know because he ululated at the window when any stray cat or dog intruded. Though he was generously tolerant of humans, he seemed to hate cats and dogs. The house and what he could see out the window was his territory. He let loose a terrible war cry to protect it.

And Snowflake could dance in the ballet mode. He was lithe and agile in a way that I could no longer be. He leaped many times the length of his stretch. He could turn in mid-flight. He was truly a wonder-cat.

Because of its enormous size the Society did not have regular meetings. A summer gathering in Hatfield Park was annually planned. Perhaps half the members showed up for it. Half was already a multitude. For real meetings, we would have had to hire a convention hall in a major city. Instead, members just seemed to convene in small informal gatherings; ten or twelve people, usually coming together by chance in the coffee shops of the town. You might find a cadre in one of the many local luncheonettes. Rosemary published a cutesy little newsletter which gave the group some cohesion. Sales of cat food and of feline accoutrement were noted weekly. You might meet ailurophiles in force at the supermarket pet supply counter when the LITTLE LITTER LETTER mentioned a bargain.

Wonderful people and crazy people made up the membership. Some of our town's most interesting citizens were part of the group -- professional people, bartenders, artists, actors, writers, poets, sportsmen, even alcoholics and lunatics and bums. For me, belonging to this group was endlessly exciting and fun.

If you saw people loitering at the benches in a park or department store or bus station or just about anywhere, odds were some ailurophiliacs were in their midst. And they talked. They loved to speak of cats. So many people had cats. And everyone complained about them. *The Beast sleeps on top of me and kneads bread on my stomach all night, claws very much in evidence. Soosanna cries to go out into the night and comes home smelling of skunk. Tuggles goes out to hunt and brings home bloody mice. Esmeralda won't catch mice at all. I suspect they could run right under her nose. Boopsie has reduced the living room furniture to shreds. Sampson knotted my knitting hopelessly. Bellybaby unfurls the toilet paper and runs it all over the house. Nougat is no fun. He sleeps twenty two hours. Then wakes up and starts negotiating for treats; Two hours of yowling and then he goes back to sleep.*

It didn't take long to realize that the complaints were usually big brags. Cat owners love the negative side of their pets. They are proud of misbehavior. I think many are so dazzled by the presence of such magnificent creatures in their very own parlors that scratches and bites are hardly felt. They become scars worn as proudly as the love bites of teen agers. *Look! Just look at what my Fluffy did to me!* becomes as loaded as *Don't tell Mama that this is what Spike did to me last night!*

They will begin grumbling about some aspect of the behavior of their special cat and end up turning it into a virtue. And it is not to be denied that there is an element of one upmanship to this eternal wrangling. Some of the most banal actions are brought forth as distinctions to be embellished upon by the next speaker. *Leonardo demands breakfast at 5 a.m.* Retort: *You have it easy. I have two furry clients awaiting breakfast at ungodly hours of the morning. When I look down from my bed I see two enormous maws, full of sharp little teeth, threatening me with extinction if*

I do not hurry up about providing sustenance. You don't know what it is to look into those spiked caverns. They are not kidding.

I joined the Ailurophiliacs at just about the time Rosemary Fingerhat released part of the roster to DOCTOR Alda Patalda, so the doctor of phonology had been making visits to some of the houses. Her study had become the subject of much discussion within the Society. Cat communication? Cat talk? Everyone accepted communication but not everyone countenanced speech. Talk was not so physically possible considering the conformation of a cat's mouth and larynx. Nevertheless I met a strange lady at the Bus Stop with a different point of view. I knew she was a fellow member because she wore a t shirt with an image of Felix. Felix the Cat, as I'm sure you all know, is a poster boy for the species *Felis domestica.* Felis for felicity -- felicity of essence and wholeness of spirit. This woman, Xanthippe Glotz was her name, maintained that her cat, Kirkwell Alexander Glotz, actually did talk, actually pronounced discernable words. She claimed he had a vocabulary of five or six words in our language. When pressed she pronounced *meat, no good, dirty* in a strange jarring voice. I presumed it to be her attempt to produce a catish accent. She sounded like the rusty hinges on an old door. The sound was jarring but performed with obvious enthusiasm, a certain admirable theatricality. By-passers all turned to stare at us. The other people on the bench headed for the curb pretending to look up and down the street for the bus.

Xanthippe was a remarkable looking woman. She had a large mane of blond hair arranged in no style in particular. It surrounded her head like a yellow bush, waving merrily with every passing breeze. She was a big woman. She had huge slanty green eyes. Everything about her was big. The Felix the Cat shirt she wore was obviously stretched to capacity to encase her large frontal works.

"That's very interesting," I said. The Society was teaching me manners. "Does Kirkwell Alexander have any phrases?"

Hereupon she let loose the longest and mightiest squeal possible to the human larynx "Ayyyyyyyiiiiiieee uuveeee ooooo ssssantiiiipf." It sounded like an alarm. It sounded like escaping steam. It sounded like murder. There was about a quart of spit in it. "That's how he says 'I love you, Xantippe.' The L and the X present difficulties but he is working on it. And the P." she said, "It's so cute how whenever he tries to make a P sound an F comes right out with it. Like this "Pffft."

More spit.

"It's so cute."

"I can see that."

I knew right then and there that no one would ever convince her otherwise. "You should get to know DOCTOR Alda Patalda," I said. "The two of you would have much to tell each other."

Xantippe Glotz and her Kirkwell Alexander Glotz, brings to my mind the subject of the naming of names. In my experience, people took great care to correctly name their cats. There were lots of members with names right out of Grade One primers – Fluffy, Tabby, Spotty. Others like Xantippe Glotz gave them serious people names. In my opinion Xantippe sounded like the name of a cat whereas Kirkwell Alexander Glotz was a name more suitable for a high school principal or the Secretary of State.

XANTIPPE GLOTZ

NAMES

Great imagination was brought to bear in the matter of naming. Snowflake was named for the wonderful shade of white that emerged after he was rescued from the bananas. Sometimes I shortened it to Flake, and that was as if ordained because there were flaky moments when, for no visible reason. he took it upon himself to race all around the house as if pursued by the coyotes. Then I just said, "Flaky's got the crazies."

The ancient gods and goddesses of the Norse, the Romans, the Greeks. Gods of ancient Babylon, heroes of the ancient books, and authors of the modern ones were among the company. Rosemary had a charming black cat named Edgar Allan Poe. He had a somber, thoughtful air. It was easy to imagine little Poe meowling out poems about ravens and pendulums and tell-tale hearts that beat terrifying tattoos up through the slats of the floor. Movie stars and gangster names were among those chosen. Domenic Tornado had one huge Maine cat called Al Capone.

When I parted from Xantippe I ran into Joe's Java Nut Café crowd where a group of ailurophiles was having more one-up discussions. It started innocently enough. Jack Fink was complaining about Myrtlemay's incurable attraction to skunks. *She comes in so stinky and, then, doesn't understand why I don't want her on my lap.*

You think that's stinky? Well, Robespierre is a long hair and, sometimes, when he does his business some of it sticks to his fur, Then he comes in and stinks the whole house up. It smells like a zoo. Just like an incontinent elephant.

Snigglefritz does a morning poop so powerful it wakes me in my bed two rooms away from the box.

Priscilla is so fastidious that one time when I was cleaning the box she popped in with a call of nature and, rather than wait, she dropped her load right in my Venetian straw gondolier's hat which was on the floor nearby. It stunk to the skies and I couldn't even try to get it back in wearable condition. Her poop is so powerful the country could use it for a weapon of war!

"Help!" I exclaimed and some of them woke up. The fact that this enlightening discussion took place over coffee and doughnuts had not seemed to phase the ailurophiliacs at all.

"What do you think of the Ailurophile Society?" Rosemary Fingerhut requested.

"A tangle of kooks," I replied.

"Good. I want you to help me untangle them a little."

"Do what?"

"Record as many cat tales as you can. Maybe we can make a book of it."

I really liked the idea. "I'll try," I said.

"Go forth and record." said Rosemary sweetly.

CATSCRATCH FEVER

This was the story Nanny Henry told me:

"On the farm there were no pets. All the animals worked. The dogs had jobs. The cats lived in the barn to catch mice and vermin. We kids were not encouraged to play with them as they could be quite wild and would as soon scratch you as drop you a curtsy. If we tangled with them once we knew to avoid them forever, except my little brother Charlie, who even got catscratch fever once from his attempt to cozy up to one of the barn cats. The tom tore up almost all the skin of Charlie's right arm. As the cuts were beginning to heal the infection came up in bunches of little pimples and Charlie got dopey and, later, lazy, wanted to sleep all the time. It took him a few months of precious childhood before he came to being the general pest and brat that he had been before.

"When he recovered he had a different attitude toward the cats. He still had enormous respect for the animals, but now he went over to watch them every day and he wrote down all their comings and goings, the things he saw them do. He claimed catscratch fever had taught him to think like a cat. He carried around a little leather bound notebook that he wouldn't let any of us touch. He gave the barn cats names which we had hitherto been reluctant to do because often they disappeared very suddenly, sometimes overnight, and that was a part of animal life that we were not eager to understand.

"Charlie said the best action was to be seen when queens had their kittens. The females manifested the most new and different behaviors. They developed a new language, a new and coaxing cry to call the young. But still, they could not count, so never noticed one missing kitten if the litter was large enough.

"One spring two of the queens produced litters. Charlie said it was impossible to tell which kitten belonged to which mama as the queens cheerfully nursed any member of the kitten population. At the same time one of the dogs littered. This particular dog, Matilda, was one who had some dealings with the cats. Not friendly, but tolerant.

"Mattie was somewhat friendly with us kids as well. Charlie did a mean thing to her. He took one of her puppies and put it in the kittening bed. The dopey little puppy didn't know the difference. When the mama cat came back she washed all the babies but not the dog baby. She pushed him to the edge of the area.

"'She didn't hurt it," Charlie said, "but it was as if she was saying 'yuk!' when it came near enough for her to smell it.'"

"Later, Charlie was able to reverse the experiment. He slipped a kitten in with the squeaking puppies. Mattie came back and nuzzled and licked the babies with no prejudice. Either she was a lot more broadminded than the cat or she was too dopey to know the difference. It was a revelation on the subject of discrimination.

"Well, there was one kitten that sort of got used to Charlie coming around. It was a dull gray color and, of course like all of the newborns, started off its life looking like a mouse. We came to call it Mousie. Mousie used to come to the edge of the barn when we were playing in the vicinity. He (or she – we never did know) would peek around to see what we were doing. Mousie also played with the puppies. That must have been forbidden by the cats' religion because it was a rare sight to us. The game they played was a chase game. First the puppy would chase Mousie, then Mousie would rear up and chase back. They could do this for quite awhile before getting dizzy and abandoning the chase.

"One day the water guy came by for an inspection. He went in the kitchen and said to our mama, 'Mrs. Henry, I think I am going to need my eyes examined. I just saw a cat chasing a dog!'

"'It's even stranger than you think,' Mama replied, 'That dog is being chased by a Mouse.'"

That remained a family joke for years.

STUPID CATS

A few ailurophiles had materialized at the B16 bus stop. As was often the case, they were bragging about their cats, but this time they were bragging about how stupid their cats were. Each participant in the discussion claimed a stupider cat than the next guy. Suddenly Mrs. Angelina Paluca appeared. She was seldom seen in town and always accompanied by one or another of her large family. She must have been waiting for her ride but the talkers made room for her on the bench. Everybody liked Mrs. P. She was very tiny and very ancient.

"When I was a child," she said, "There was no such thing as commercial pet food. Pets ate table scraps and just hoped for something palatable. In our house it was left over pasta and you know the animals could only hope for a meat or fish sauce. That was very rarely the case as times were hard and meat cost a packet.

"We lived in a nice but poor neighborhood. It wasn't so bad because everyone was poor in those days. When houses stood empty there was no one to buy them. They soon became derelict. Just such a derelict house stood right next to ours. It soon became a playground for rowdy boys and mice.

"My mama took care of the rowdy boys. She'd give them a good bawling out and threaten to call their parents. That was a threat that worked in those days. But she was afraid of mice, deathly afraid. She had a mouse phobia. Soon some of the mice challenged the frontiers and showed signs of invading our house where at least there was the possibility of food. This is when Mama got the bright idea to bring in a cat.

"Except for extra toes, the cat she brought in was a nondescript alley type whom we children named Spunky. Mama said cats with extra toes were better mousers and, indeed, Spunky did her job excellently well. We thought her beautiful: she gave full satisfaction. The only drawback to this addition to our family was that Spunky was an intact female.

"Before long the inevitable happened. Spunky gave birth to two babies. One looked exactly like her mother and, not very imaginatively, we called her Spunky Junior. The other was a little black and white male. The boy had a splotch of black on the top of his head and we called him Top Hat.

"It soon became apparent that Top Hat was really stupid. Spunky and Spunky Junior seemed well aware of his lack of brains. They had to protect him from everything. When he went to jump, he miscalculated and plopped on the floor with none of the usual grace we expected of the cats. You could almost see Spunky and Spunky Junior going 'Tch, tch, tch,' to each other.

"Spunky was a fabulous mother. She brought little crickets and bugs and showed Spunky Junior what do about them. Top Hat would watch in confused bafflement. He just didn't get it. When the food dish came out Top Hat was so dopey that it would be almost empty before he got in close enough to eat. But he did love food. He did love to eat.

"As I said, there was no special food for pets in those days, but Mama was friends with the butcher, and on rare occasions he would give her scraps of the organ meats that most American people wouldn't touch. We were not so destitute as to crave gut stew, but the cats did love it. Top Hat would go especially crazy for lungs. When he smelled lungs he would do a lung dance and sing a lung song. It was a real picnic to see his shenanigans.

"To Mama's despair, right alongside our house there crumbled away one of those abandoned houses I mentioned earlier. One fine morning in May we heard a terrible sound. It was Top Hat, in distress. Somehow he had gotten into the abandoned house and worked his way to the upstairs porch. There he sat singing his desolate song. Spunky and Spunky Junior were going nuts. The upstairs porch, parallel to ours, was much too high. The cat didn't know how to get down! He was too stupid to figure out going back the way he had come. All he knew to do was cry.

"He cried all night. The next morning he was still up there, crying mournfully.

"'He's such a dope!' I said. ''The others would have figured something out for sure.'

""Let's try something,' Papa said. He got a wide plank and laid it so it formed a bridge from our top porch to the neighboring one.

"No dice. Top Hat would not cross. No amount of encouragement helped. He was scared. Papa got a long pole and sent me to Sal Perricone's shop. I returned with neat little bag of entrails which Papa attached to the pole and plunked on to the bridge where the famished Top Hat could smell it. He responded with heart breaking cries. Little by little, Papa moved the guts closer to us. Surely half-starved, Top Hat, very tentatively, crossed the bridge to our top porch where he crouched enjoying a feast that he so rarely got.

"'What a stupid cat,' I said to Papa.

"To our surprise, a few days later we heard, again, the frightful sound of a desperate cat. It was Top Hat. He had trapped himself again. Now we knew the solution. We got the plank. Laid across the two porches it made a broad enough route for any normal cat but Top Hat was not a normal cat. He just cried, and the sight of the plank only made him cry the harder. Again I was ordered to Sal's butcher shop. And, again, the scene of coaxing followed by delirious joy and voracious gobbling ensued.

"'What a stupid cat,' I said to Papa.

"'You think so?' Papa replied."

THE WANDERING MINSTREL

Apache Heights had a terrible problem. Something came meandering through the yards every night screaming its lungs out. It was a terrible scream, demanding attention. A wild animal, people thought, but not a familiar one or, at least, not emitting a familiar cry. This disturbance continued most of the night with few pauses and it moved all over the yards of the residents. It could not quite be located. Everyone was frantic with the borderline madness that arises from loss of sleep. "I ain't slept a wink since eternity," complained Trudy Wack. "Somebody get Herb!"

Herb Buggmeister was a great big man who for reasons of social sorting everyone in Apache Heights recognized as their leader. And Herb was just as furious as everyone else. He really liked his sleep. That nocturnal screaming reverberated in his thalamus and even distressed his back teeth. Herb, a man of action always, resolved to catch the creature and deal with it. "I'll wring its frigging neck," he declared.

Many agreed with him. A committee of the sleep-deprived formed to help him.

"We'll get him, Herb," they promised.

"Don't touch a hair of his head, if he has hair on his head," Herb warned. "I want to be the one to deliver the punishment! I'll tear its head, if it has a head, right off its neck. If it has a neck, that is."

Among the residents of Apache Heights there was the usual percentage of ailurophiles, and they were alarmed. It disturbed them to hear about the possible punishments that Herb intended to wreak on an animal that might turn out to be a cat. Well, even if it was not a cat, it ran counter to their philosophy to harm its frigging neck or any other part of its frigging body. If it had a frigging body.

They sent for Rosemary Fingerhat.

Rosemary had an old friendship with Herb Buggmeister. They had dated in high school. She counted on those memories of sweeter days to soften the big fellow up. "Please, Herb," she said. "Don't do anything violent."

"The hell you say, Ro," replied Herb. "It's kept this whole community suffering for more than a week now and I am going to exact slow punishment for that."

"Slow punishment?" someone muttered. "He means torture!" The terrible word "torture" was running around among the gathering residents who were, after all and at most times, a peaceful assemblage, when suddenly a cry was heard from Herb's posse.

"We got him, Herb!"

"What the hell kind of varmint is it?" yelled Herb, There was blood lust in his voice.

It was just a cat. Just a sad looking scared cat.

Rosemary rushed before Herb's minions could. The culprit was not only an ordinary house cat but it wore a collar which identified it as property of the Liederkrantz family of this same neighborhood. Rosemary immediately took the carrier and went to see Sonita Liederkrantz, who had much to answer for.

Sonita was abject. Yes, the cat was theirs. What bothered him she did not know but Sonita claimed he howled all day and more at night especially as the moon rose. She just had to let him out at night because of the babies. She had babies. Too many bratty babies too close in age. The babies could not sleep with that alarm going off all night.

"He must have a reason for behaving this way," said Rosemary as she carted the carrier back out where Herb's adherents snatched it and delivered it to the porch of the Buggmeister house. There Herbert awaited with murder in his eye. He claimed the cage with a victor's cry.

Interested onlookers crowded around. Silence reigned. Out of the middle of the murderous mob and amid the suspended breaths thereof a very tiny woman who was Mrs. Herbert Buggmeister emerged. In the manner of some very big men, Herb had married and doted upon the smallest woman in the town, Florrie Buggmeister, an avowed ailurophile.

"Put that down, Herbert!" she demanded. "You're not going to do any harm to that cat!"

"But, Sweetcheeks …"

"Let it out of the cage," said Florrie Buggmeister, "Now!"

Someone unhooked the door of the carrier and the woebegone cat stepped out daintily.

There was a terrible quiet on the porch. All eyes were on Herb now. And on the cat. Like at a ping pong game the observing eyes went back and forth.

Out onto the hushed porch plodded a new participant, MonaLisa Buggmeister, Herb Buggmeister's prize English bulldog. She was a massive bitch and she trudged onto the porch where all the action was playing out.

"Okay, Mona. You do it! Take apart that damned cat!" Herb shouted.

But Mona didn't. Instead she approached and sniffed a very hydraulic sniff. The cat arched his back and purred. Mona gave him some wet kisses. It was a weird scene and everyone acknowledged it as a sort of sign from above.

"How sweet! Let that be a lesson to all of you," said Florrie, supposedly to the assembled posse. Then, to Herb, "Darling, I want to keep him!" Ever a one to sway to her wishes, Herb agreed.

"I'm going to call him Pavarotti," Florrie announced.

FAT CATS

There are some problems that can raise a flap among ailurophiles at any time. First and most heinous is the subject of declawing. Most cat lovers abhor this practice and compare it to the removal of a few human knuckles. Yet there are those who will indulge in declawing for the sake of their overstuffed sofa. In shame, they hide their perfect drawing rooms and hope no one notices the unmarred chairs and fluffed divans that have escaped cruel depredations.

Another dangerous subject is freedom of range. Should the cats wander free or not? There is plenty of room for debate here as there is plenty of reason for debate. Cars and coyotes have no respect for wandering felines. Sometimes large birds may be looking for a dinner entre in the local gardens. Nature will prevail so there is also the question of cats targeting the bird feeders. Nevertheless, wandering cats are to be seen in our neighborhood. They have begged or spirited themselves out the door because they love their freedom.

And then there is the fat question. Fat cats growing fatter and fatter is another notable problem of the new era. The sight of a fatty is enough to raise a chorus of disapproval. And there are so many of them! Overfeeding's a much more common offense than declawing or allowing free passage into the dangers of the night. Fatties waddled around everywhere. It is a common situation and becoming more prevalent as more yummy treats for cats are concocted by the ever-grasping cat food companies.

People love their cats. Cats love treats. Some faint hearts simply can not be meowed at without presenting a tidbit. Meow. Another. Meow! And yet another. You, know, cats can meow as if their hearts will break. Treats ensue. Beloved cats balloon into dirigibles, plain blimpses.

Stories of fat cats abounded. Hortense Bumpas, beloved pet of Elmer and Dorris Bumpas for example, had the most pathetic meow in the world. She could sound like the most tragic diva in the history of feline dramatics. Deprived and neglected, she would keep up the lament until her owner would provide a treat. Then Hortense might sniff it, see if it passed her strict requirements, and either gobble it or waddle away with her little pink nose in the air. Naturally, if rejected, Dorris would feel the rebuff, sometimes enough to present another, different treat. Keep providing treats until accepted. That was the name of the game. Do I need to tell you, Hortense was as fat as a pig? And she loved Elmer Bumpas more than life itself. In the night she would leap her full corporosity onto to his delicate stomach.

Rosemary Fingerhat told me that in the days when she was dating her late husband, who was also an ailurophile, he had three fat female cats, collectively referred to as the Girls or the Sisterhood. In the evening Paul Fingerhat had the habit of coming home from his job, plopping into the La-Z-boy chair, and stretching out to enjoy the news on television. The cats, all of them plus sizes, would arrange themselves on Paul's supine body. Their combined weight was formidable. He was then immobilized by love, a slave to ailurophilia. If, when the newscast was over, Paul made as if to move, the cats resented it. He got some spitting and low throat murmurs that were not nice at all.

"Give 'em the boot, Paul," Rosemary advised. "Give 'em a flying lesson. Let 'em know who's boss."

"But they spit, Honey. I don't want them to hate me."

It was thus, one evening long ago, that Paul Fingerhat invented the world's first remote control. He found a long tree branch in the garden and with it he could reach to poke the television controls enough to change channels or switch off. This was considered so clever by Paul and so funny by Rosemary that she decided then and there to marry the man. "He loved cats, you know, Skinny Malinck. He couldn't stand for them to spit at him. The worst punishment that ever came out of him was to shout, 'Move yer fat ass, Sister!' which had no effect whatsoever."

Paul's cats were very verbal. They could produce meows of incredible volume and they did for almost any situation they did not approve. Paul couldn't bear these squalls and don't for a minute think they didn't know it. They also had amazing manual dexterity. If you looked at their paws they were only the usual little round pads with round button toes. No telling how these clumsy little tools could do what they did, but the Sisters hated closed doors and they had studied the nature of closures enough to figure out some tricks of aperture. To open the cabinets they lay on their backs and batted their forepaws against the edge until they succeeded in whacking it open. The bedroom door required a trick. Patty, the fattest Sister, would raise herself up to put her weight against the door while LaVerne and Maxine sprang the knob. First, of course, they gave loud warning. Rosemary was loathe to use the bathroom in Paul's house as the closed door seemed to be a challenge. She feared she might be exposed at any moment.

Another peculiarity of the three fat cats was that they were puritanical prudes. Though Paul and Rosemary were at the tenderest beginnings of their love they were not permitted to express these feelings at all. If they sat too close together on the couch three fat ladies began butting them, sitting on them, generally pestering the couple, even going so far as to give little bites to the fingers and meowing loudly and disapprovingly into their ears.

All's well that ends well and when Rosemary married Paul things began to calm down. The resentment of the fat girls ceased entirely as they realized they now had two servants instead of one.

HIGH NAMES AND SNOOTY NOSES

Provenance is always a favorite topic for ailurophile discussions. Last Friday three of the most elevated members were sitting on the bench at Johnson's Farm where an array of hummingbird feeders had been hung for the delight and delectation of onlookers. But these guys were not discussing hummingbirds. They had high class cats and they wanted everyone to know about it.

"I had to wait almost a year for my Alouette." said Rodney Bloomer. "We got her from a cattery in New Mexico that specializes in Egyptian Maus. We had to go through the whole pregnancy. Then, with bated breath, attended the birth by telephone connection because we could get no closer. We did succeed in getting the breeder to videotape the birth because we needed that intimate connection with our little girl.

"And the resemblance to the ancient line is unmistakable. She is an ancient Egyptian, lean and graceful with a pair of ears that swing out to double the size of her head when they are fully unfurled. She is the joy of my life."

"Do you have any children, Rodney," I asked.

"Yes, three daughters, and they are just as crazy about Alouette as I am."

"And your wife?"

He gave me his somber look. "No, I'm sorry to say she is not. But she would be were it not for Alouette's tendency to spit at her."

"It's really hard to like someone that spits at you," I remarked.

"I think Louise should try harder. Alouette has strong affections and disaffections, she comes by it honestly. It's a hallmark of the breed."

I noticed that his wife, once a regular at ailurophile gatherings, had recently ceased to make any appearances at these park side brag fests. "Would be good for domestic tranquility if she would soften her view but I guess if Alouette spits at her it is difficult."

"Alouette won't change, so Louise must!" Rodney proclaimed with full male obstinacy.

"Oh-oh," thought I. "A marriage rocked by a cat. It's a real catastrophe. I must tell Rosemary. Maybe she can soften Rodney, if not Alouette."

Not to be outdone, Harvey Plunk, who owns the Ford dealership in town, chimed in, "We waited a few <u>years</u> for our Tonkinese."

"Tonkinese? Is it a breed? I never heard of it."

"Of course not. Very rare," he announced. "He's a pure darling. He's a blue-eyed, champagne colored Tonkinese, and he loves everyone in the household and everyone out of it. Even common visitors and tradespeople are always treated to his greetings and affection."

"Even if they can't stand cats?" I asked politely.

"Well. yes, since you mention it. Especially if they don't like cats. Cat haters get his special affection. He is like a missionary of the cat creed, out to change people's ailurophobia to ailurophilia. He'll get right into their laps and start loving them. Licking and giving little bite kit-kisses as well. If they close up their laps to him he has been known to drape himself on their shoulders."

"Has he made any converts?"

"Not yet," said Harvey sheepishly. "As a matter of fact, a few of our good friends have quit coming over. We lost my best buddy who is morbidly allergic to cats. He can't even stand to sit next to me in the car. He says I reek of cat. My wife says 'The hell with those poops. Who needs them?'"

"Who does need them?"

"Me, a little," said Harvey sadly. "Whelan was my best golf buddy."

"A shame and a pity, but all is not always roses in the gardens of Felis cattus," I said.

Dolores Twerper sidled up to get in her song of praise. She had a Turkish Van cat that she claimed would jump into the fish pool in the yard to have itself a little swim. She had taken pictures of this phenomenon which she carried at all times in case her audience tried to give her the lie. The cat had markings like a great big bushy Turkish moustache. She called the guy Mustafa, and claimed he was mean as a viper. "They are a rare breed," Dolores claimed. "They live on the shores of Lake Van. Perhaps for that reason, the kitties like to take a swim now and then, though the waters of Lake Van are highly alkaline and very few fish can survive in it. Maybe Mustafa is seeking that alkaline wash which his ancestors so enjoyed. He is a very prized and rare cat even in his own country.

"When I first moved here I first let Mustafa out into the garden. Suddenly I heard an awful sound cry from the bushes, a sort of rattle. At the same time all the birds flew out of the bush. I saw Mustafa backing out of the shadows. He had made himself fat as a pasha and was preparing to do battle with the rattler, as rattler I believe it was. I had to call him away."

"Bet he was glad to come."

"What kind of cat is yours, Skinny Malinck?" asked Rodney Fried.

"Just a craven, pusillanimous pure white cattus vulgarus bananicus," I replied proudly.

"Bananicus?"

"Yes. Bananicus does seem to have had something to do with it," I assured them proudly.

When at a later date Rosemary and I tried to tally up our long and ever-growing list of Ailurophile members, I reported the sad case of Louise Bloomer who had left the Society because of the spitting of a prize Egyptian Mau. Rosemary was as saddened as I was by the loss of any contributing members. She remembered Louise as previously active, the creator of tiny rain boots for cats which had been regularly advertised in the KITTY LITTER LETTER even though no one ever bought them.

"Cats don't spit just for fun. There has to be a reason. Might just be a question of smell."

Rosemary took it upon herself to pay a visit to the Bloomer house where her nasal investigations proved Louise to be the essence of ritz. "You know, Skinny," she reported. "The woman is so hoity toity she only wears $90 perfumes. She slathers it on because she has no sense of smell to tell her when to stop. The one she was wearing the day I stopped by was called Jungle Passion. 'Lose the jungle passion,' I told her. I recommended a potion I brew myself. It combines essence of catnip with casein solids and a whisper of liver. One whiff of the stuff and Alouette began to romp and play drunkenly. Both Louise and Alouette were genuinely delighted."

So peace was restored to the Bloomer household. Later, however, Louise was heard to complain that, in moments of the wildest affection, Alouette had a tendency to nibble rather too passionately on her ear.

THREE FREE SPIRITS

Purrsy

Some cats can never be tamed to the hearth. The wild night and the wild outdoors will always call them away from cozy comforts and into ways that can only be walked alone. Such was the case with Purrsy.

Early on a Tuesday morning Eleanora Philpotts first noticed that some kind of trespasser had invaded her enclosed patio. Someone had disturbed the dish of seeds she left on the table for the birds. It could have been a large bird but the seeds were not eaten, just stirred about. The mystery was solved later that same day when she looked out and saw a great big grayish tomcat sitting on that very table staring at her. He was immobile, possibly waiting for some poor bird to come in for a seed snack.

The concentrated stare startled Ellie. Since childhood she had not had any dealings with cats. This one seemed to her to be huge. Another question that bothered her -- how ever did the creature get on her patio? The wall was high, not impossibly high but high enough to give Ellie privacy from the street. Perhaps not too high for this giant feline to vault over. That must have been what had happened, Ellie thought. She thought he looked dirty and disreputable enough to ignore all human barriers. Disturbingly he continued to stare. He had his green eyes trained on her for almost an hour. She continued on household tasks awhile. When she looked again the cat was gone.

On Wednesday at about noon Eleanora looked out and saw the cat on the table again. He was looking at her fixedly but he didn't make a sound. She meant to watch to see how he would leave but time slipped by. The trespasser was gone again before she realized.

By Thursday her curiosity was aroused. This cat came every day to stare at her. Did he have a purpose? She stared back and studied him closely. He was very majestic, imperial in his attitude, but really quite filthy. Now she could discern he was skeletal. Ellie was a kind hearted woman and the condition of the cat disturbed her greatly. She thought she could count his bones. Next day she consulted with ailurophile friends to learn the proper foods to feed a starving cat. She surprised herself in this. She had never had intentions of becoming a cat owner.

Tentatively she opened the door to the patio intending to put a little dish of food out there for the cat but the marauder pushed right past, emitting a loud purr the minute he crossed the threshold. He sashayed into the kitchen, purring as he came, louder and louder. That purr was the first sound she had heard from him. Heretofore he had not even once meowed.

"Hmmm," she mused. "He must belong to someone. He seems to know what a kitchen is for." She put the little dish on the kitchen floor and the cat sniffed it thoroughly before he calmly ate the contents. "He may be half starved but he has his dignity," Ellie thought.

"Okay. You're welcome. Goodbye now," said Ellie but the cat had different ideas. He decided to take a tour of the house. There were a few soft surfaces that called to him. He tried them all, purring loudly. He took several small naps and would then resume his explorations. "It's okay," Ellie thought. "Eventually he'll go out and maybe even find his original home again." But the cat just purred and roamed about. He seemed very pleased with his surroundings. During these explorations he finally jumped on to Ellie's lap where he gave a demonstration of delight and a loud purr concert. "I might keep you," Ellie said. "If only you weren't so dirty."

So she let him stay. She was heartened when he went into the bathroom. She heard splashing and ran in. Could he be having a wash? No. All he did was lean his long body over the commode for a deep drink. This was somewhat appalling to Ellie. No. He was just making a mess. Apparently he saw an imaginary fish or something in the commode and was splashing away at it. He soon desisted. "Cats are supposed to wash themselves," Ellie reminded him. "Aren't they?"

He purred.

She called him Purrsy.

As the day grew long Purrsy began trying to open the patio door. Ellie was against it. She knew how dangerous the great outdoors was for wandering cats. There were cars and coyotes and even birds of prey. Just that very morning someone told her that the men who retiled the roof of the SuperX found cat bones up there, the leavings of big predator birds. No amount of persuasion would deter Purrsy in his determination to get out.

She worried about him all night.

There he was the next morning, sitting among the seeds, just as dirty and determined as ever. He entered jauntily, but purring happily as Ellie opened the door.

In the next few days he lived at Ellie's house, disreputable and loving, demanding to go out each night. After about a week Purrsy went and stayed gone. Ellie was disconsolate. Rosemary Fingerhat stopped by to console her. "He could have become coyote food," Ellie moaned.

"Probably not," Rosemary assured her. "He was a big guy that knew the score. He was never a possession. Think of him as a special guest."

Mr. Whiskers

Linda Schmutz lived in a crowded area out near the airport. Her garden was small but precious. On the weekends she loved to potter around in the new laid flower beds. One day a cat entered and with interest and curiosity observed her efforts. Linda was not especially pleased. Though she did not like cats she was, generally speaking, an animal lover. She was still mourning her beloved dog, Whiskers, when she saw the cat. The cat was a worrisome sight, bedraggled, not your Sunday picture of a cat. She chased him vigorously out of the yard by shouting loud *SCATS!* at him.

Morty, her neighbor, looked over the fence.

"You got the cat, Kiddo," he said.

"Not me, Morty. I just don't want him digging in the flower beds."

"He don't dig. He don't cry. He's just hungry."

That made Linda sad. She knew what a driving force hunger could be. During her student days she had survived on a can of soup and some saltine crackers for a whole week. Hunger was painful. As she busied herself with the flowers she discerned a shadow beyond the fence. There was a small, silent black and white onlooker. She was being watched. "Oh, okay, Cat. Just don't dig in here."

But the cat wasn't digging. He was hiding from her. She went in the kitchen and found some left over meatloaf which she crumbled. When she went out again the cat was hiding behind the fence slats. "Whiskers liked this," she said. "Do you?" She put the offering down on a piece of paper. The cat didn't move. Linda walked to the far end of the garden and the cat came slinking toward the meat, which made Linda sad, and even sadder when she saw with what ravenous hunger the poor creature attacked the crumbs of meat. "I like you, Mister," she said. "But I don't want you. Once in a while I'll give you a treat. If you don't mind I'll call you Mr. Whiskers, after my dog."

Later Morty came back to the fence. "You fed him, didn't you?"

"I felt sorry."

"You're a big softy, Lin. Now he'll come back all the time."

But he didn't and she looked for him. One day she called. "Mr. Whiskers! Mr. Whiskers!" in a loud and screechy voice. She saw the black and white cat come creeping toward the fence as if he knew his name. He did not come to the food until she moved back away from it. Linda laughed. "You learned your name real fast, Mister Whiskers."

From that time on he came if she called him with the loud and screechy voice. Their relationship continued several years. Then Mr. Whiskers vanished.

"Where's your cat?" Morty asked.

"He went away."

"Bet he was scrunched by a car."

"Bet not," Linda said defensively. "He went away. That's all. Mr. Whiskers was a survivor."

Attila

There were some subjects guaranteed to rile the blood of true ailurophiles. One was the surgical removal of claws. True, there were some society members who had had this intervention done on their cats to preserve the integrity of priceless rugs or furniture. Those who had it done usually kept quiet about it. Rosemary Fingerhat abhorred the practice. "Can they compare a dumb lazy boy to a living creature? What have they got anyhow in their friggin' houses anyhow -- priceless Medieval tapestries?"

Even more reprehensible was the occasional tampering with genetic material or imaginative breeding. Because there was money involved in such experimentation there were those who would fool with the nature of animals and produce genetic freaks. A beautiful hybrid could be of commercial value though frequently at war with its own body. Many did not care. Such people prized the individual look of their animals more than their personalities, feelings or karma.

There appeared a cat around our neighborhood, a stray and a rover who had the look of a tiger. It was in size and shape an ordinary cat, but it was decorated with the marks of the wild. It had actual stripes. Such an unusual animal must be worth something. We thought it must have escaped from somewhere, or someone had had to throw it out because it acted so fierce. It snarled when approached. For a while this animal hung about in our area traumatizing all the good people. Even before striking a blow it gained the name Attila, like the Scourge of God.

Attila took particular interest in the dogs. Methodically he searched the yards and alleyways seeking out every big dog in residence. Owners of small dogs soon realized they had best put the squeakers away. They would serve Attila as no more than potato chips. There were some big dogs in our area. There were pit bulls and great danes and every sort of big or medium canine. Attila would swoop down and challenge them. His trick was to swipe his murderous paw right across the nose. The conflict ended as a yelping dog cowered away into a corner. Attila asked no more.

This went on for about a week while we discussed what might be done. Then after all this stir and confusion Attila disappeared. Several neighbors said they saw him walking off into the desert. It was to be assumed that he was on the search for coyotes to discipline.

ANTONIO

After Purrsy went adventuring into the night Eleanora Philpotts continued peering out into the garden. She had not been so crazy about the dirty old hobo but in some way he had gotten under her skin. She found she missed him. He had made an ailurophile of her so when the demise of her friend Jason Twitch resulted in an orphaned cat Elly agreed to take him.

Antonio was a big white cat as clean as Purrsy had been dirty. Ellie was enchanted by his candid blue eyes. She thought he must be Siamese or at least part Siamese and this was proved true by voice. Antonio's voice was invasive and it soon developed that he knew how to use it.

From the start Elly, cognizant of those cat bones on the roof of the SuperX, realized that there were too many dangers in the streets and byways. She couldn't bear to lose another cat as she had lost Purrsy. Elly decided Antonio was to be a house cat. But did he agree? For all the time he had been sharing quarters with Jason Twitch, Antonio had been free to roam. He was a denizen of the night, the hero of who knows what adventures in the darkness.

The minute the first evening of cohabitation with Elly began, Antonio became restless. He marched around from window to window clearly making his desires known. Soon he began to sing. The song turned into a demand. He thrashed against the windows. He bumped into Elly's legs. His cry was terrible. He was clearly miserable and Elly, though she stayed resolute, decided she must do something about alleviating his pain. So began a series of gentle experiments until Antonio learned, through love and determination, to walk with Elly. He walked on a leash but not as your doggy does. He walked like a cat. That is, he stopped whenever he wanted to and for as long as he wanted to. With loving patience, Elly waited. The neighbors soon became accustomed to the sight of Elly and cat. "Is Antonio taking you for a walk again?" they would call out to her.

But it wasn't so simple. Antonio was now used to having an afternoon walk each day. When it wasn't forthcoming he demanded it with his loudest operatic wail. "MeOUT," he cried. If the leash did not soon appear his cry would escalate into a *fortissimo appassionato*.

"MeOUT!

"Mee **OUT!**

"**MEEE OWWWT!**"

"**NEE-OW!**"

ELLIE PHILPOTTS AND ANTONIO

MEHITABEL

There was a deep mystery attached to the old asylum building on Horse Chestnut Hill. The place had been boarded up since 1967 when finances and scandal forced its closure. It was supposedly supervised by guards who came by only sporadically. Maybe not at all, since there was little traffic on Chestnut Hill. But there was certainly activity there. The town knew that. Comings and goings, lights, strange sounds. The place had such a terrible reputation that few dared approach except for a little gang of street urchins led by Peggy Malarky, the terror of St. Agnes School.

The grounds of the old neglected sanatorium were overgrown but perfect for a throng of rowdy kids. There were trees to climb and tall grasses that hid creeping children. In addition there was the aura of lunacy, of screaming maniacs that lurked on the premises and gave just the right impetus to send shivers of delight up the spines of the marauding boys and girls. They frequently saw and heard things they knew could not possibly be there. The cat that inhabited those spaces added to the charm of the place. She could be counted on to jump out from nowhere, land right on the shoulders of some surprised child who would indulge in yelling bloody murder. No one ever caught her though she ran atop heads and rode shoulders frequently. She could not be caught or petted or talked to as can a normal kitty. They decided she embodied the soul of one of the wretched lunatics who had died such miserable deaths in the institution over the years. They called her Mehitabel.

The kids had figured this much out: it was Father Donnelly who came up in the heart of night, braving the demons of the demented souls that lingered there. Father went up only at night. They realized the time frame because they were only brave enough to go up in the afternoon light. Obviously, Father D. had crepuscular business. What it could be demanded their attention. Priests were as likely to get into mischief as anyone else. If they had exorcisms why could they not have séances, calling demons instead of chasing them? Peggy Malarky tried to convince the children that they had to know. But no one shared her reckless curiosity. This was in the huge and empty refectory which the children had finally succeeded in entering only just that afternoon. At one sniff of the place and a studied look around, Peggy had a pretty good idea of what went had been there. In spite of the evidence of her senses she was mystified. She contrived to linger after all the others left and she secreted herself in an alcove to await the arrival of the priest. There were echoes and strange shadows and, of course, that unmistakable smell.

Peggy kept low.

But it was not easy. The place was monumentally spooky. The wind made terrible noises going around the old building. Several times Peggy thought her heart would stop. She thought of abandoning her mission but something stubborn inside her would not let her desist. In the middle of tremors and shivers she felt something dreadful brush her cheek. What was it? A clump of spider webs? There came after it a piercing meow. It was the tail of the cat, Mehitabel. At the same moment the enormous double doors of the refectory gave a loud squeak and opened to the night. A horse walked in! Polly shivered and heard her own teeth rattle. She thought her heart would burst. The cat grabbed the top of her skull and she gave an audible little squawk of surprise, even though her nose had already informed her of horse presence.

Closing the door behind the horse, Father Donnelly entered the huge, echoing room.

Mehitabel was meowing loudly and, at risk of her skin and hands, Polly began petting her. Unaccustomed as she was to actual touch, this handling only made her louder. Now she was yowling. Father Donnelly certainly noticed and he turned a flashlight on the strange sight of Peggy Malarky with a cat on her head. "Who might you be?" he said.

"Peggy Malarky, Father," she replied.

"Do you like horses?"

"Yes, Father."

"I'd like to give him to you."

"Excuse me, Father Donnelly?"

"Take a lesson, Peggy. Gambling is complicated. I won this beast and now I don't know what to do with him. You can have him if you want him."

"Oh, no, Father. My dad won't let a pet in the house. Not even a goldfish."

"See here, girl. You'd best be out of here. I am going to barter this horse with the devil this night. If you don't want me to barter you off as well, you'd best be gone and never gabble about what you saw or heard here tonight."

"Yes, Father, yes!" she agreed.

"Now. Get that creature off your head and get out of here before the devil sees you!"

Peggy wasn't afraid of much but she was mortally afraid of the devil. Tight caught now in Peggy's scalp, Mehitabel was drawing blood. At the foot of the hill Peggy succeeded in freeing herself. She began jogging home. The cat was right behind her. Apparently it had been traumatized by the events of the evening too. It followed her every step down that hill.

The creature entered her home at her feet. She could not catch it to evict it, so she shut the door and tiptoed to her bed. Her dad would be coming home from his Friday night libations soon and she wanted to be asleep when he came in.

Mehitabel took off on explorations.

At about two in the morning a mighty scream rent the air. "Christ and the Saints preserve us! We're under attack by the British!" Right in his bed, Mehitabel had attached herself to Daddy's skull. He shook her off. He thought she'd been detached by his evocation of the saints. He could not send her away.

They reconciled and became the best of friends. For the many years until he died Pa Malarky wore Mehitabel around his neck, like a scarf.

APOLLONIA

I love my friends but some of them are certifiable. For example, Deena Dingles phoned this morning. She asked for the number of the vet I called when Snowflake, my mini cat, had the vapors. "I need someone special. Someone with the sensitivity required to help Apollonia with a very intimate problem," she announced. I could tell by the tone of her voice that I had best refrain from levity.

"What! What? Whatever can be troubling your little Polly, Dee?" I asked. Deena doesn't care for it but I like to shorten the names of her cats. The last one was Clytemnestra. Not a name of fortunate augury. Most of us could not get our tongue around Clytemnestra and no nickname seemed appropriate so she ended up being called "Clyde" by Dee's friends. Apollonia was easier. Polly would work.

"It's terrible, Skinny. I think my Apollonia is a nymphomaniac!"

I was quiet for a full minute before I could react. "Deena, don't tell me she has never been spayed."

"Oh, of course she has. I had the little darling fixed when I first got her. Dr. Woo did it, and he is supposed to be the most prestigious veterinarian in town."

"Please tell me, Dee. What in the world makes you think she's a nympho?"

"She keeps …" Dee hesitated. Obviously the subject was quite painful to her. "I tell you, Skinny, she keeps *presenting*. You know how female cats do when they're in heat? Dogs too. Well, that's exactly it. She keeps *presenting herself.*"

I tried to understand. "Presenting herself to other cats, Dee? I thought you kept her strictly alone, a single cat. Do you have other cats around?"

"I thank my lucky stars I do not! Imagine the riot that would cause! Apollonia is a house cat. She never goes out, and I do *not* keep other cats. She's an only child.

"I can tell by your voice that you are not taking this seriously, Skinny," she admonished. "I am *telling* you, and I want you to take this seriously. She just keeps *presenting* herself. To *everything*. She started with an elaborate invitation to the big ottoman in the family room. I was astonished but, you know, it is at least covered with fur. Fake fur, I guess. Furry stuff anyhow. I thought it was some kind of atavistic antagonism. Feline behavior of some kind. But normal. Maybe territorial aggression. I did not at first perceive the significance of her motions. But then she really went crazy. Before long she was presenting herself to everything. To me. To the magazine rack. To Barry's golf bag out in the foyer. Hiram Loony came by, bringing documents for Barry to sign, and Apollonia made an amorous advance to Hiram's shoes. It was something to behold. Her meaning was unmistakable, lowering and dragging her hindquarters seductively while she sang that godawful song of unrequited love."

"Poor Apollonia. I know just how she must feel."

"Don't try to be funny, Skinny Malinck," Deena reprimanded. "This is not only serious but it's potentially damned embarrassing. I'm hosting the bridge club tomorrow. That's bad enough but imagine if someone like Barry's mother drops by. I regret to say she often does. Drop by, that is. Apollonia might just sashay in, presenting herself hither and thither to every briefcase and stray galosh in sight."

I found it hard to contain myself. "No real danger, there, Dee. I doubt if Apollonia could get in the family way from your mother-in-law's galoshes."

"Skinny, it is not funny -- the presenting and the caterwauling. She sounds in pain."

"I dare say we've all known that pain. Did you call your usual vet?"

"Dr. Woo's a jackass. He must have done the process wrong in the first place and, when I told him about the situation, he laughed for about fifteen minutes."

"And?"

"And he said maybe the original surgery was incomplete. He gave me an appointment for next week and told me to pop her."

"Pop her?"

"Pop her with a pencil!" she announced with audible indignation.

"Well, give her my condolences. Deena, I think what you really need is a cat psychologist. Polly sounds deprived, like most of the women we know. I'm afraid there just aren't enough pencils in the civilized world."

Dee hung up on me.

Apollonia

GUSTAFF – EXPLORER

1984-2005

Rosemary Fingerhat has asked me to collect some cat tales to include in her little newsletter. It was the easiest assignment I ever had. The members were so forthcoming with the adventures of their felines. One had only to ask, "Is there anything special or unusual about your cat?" to see their eyes light up with the remembrance of feats or eccentricities new to the chronicles of catdom.

Annamary Twitter told me about about Gustaff, a speckled male of the alley variety, that she and her roommate, Evelyn Pygg, acquired on a rainy night in Boston. They found him in a puddle. He was a little more than a kitten but already had scars to demonstrate an active love life. He was a bedraggled, ragged little bum. But, in the way of cats, it took him no time at all to realize that he had now acquired the kind of privileges he deserved. Gustaff grew accustomed to luxury as soon as he awoke in their nice dry house. He seemed happy to have a permanent home and two new servants to cater to his needs. Service was given with love as Gustaff knew how to reward attention with affection. His purring was positively orchestral.

When they moved to the wild west Gustaff was accorded many more opportunities to explore the world. The women took him along when they went camping. Once he got lost in Monument Valley. They called and called. They were frantic. Finally like Indian scouts of old they followed his tracks right up to the dangerous rocks they could not climb. Fortunately, Gustaff heard and descended.

But again, when they made a rest stop, he went on a solitary exploration. Again they called but this time to no avail. Gustaff was gone and it was getting late. They had to get a move to set up camp before dark. They proceeded to a campsite about 30 miles up the road. That night they hardly slept at all. They felt they had abandoned the guy and right alongside a busy highway. In the morning they retraced their route. At the previous night's rest spot they parked. They had not long to wait before they heard a wailing cry. It was Gustaff, crouched in the grass in the median beside the road. He ran to rejoin them. He purred a triumphant concerto. The boy knew very well where his next meal was coming from.

By the time they moved to our community Gustaff had reached the advanced age of seventeen years. Senility was beginning to be apparent. They could see the faltering in his movements. He had lost the agility and his sureness of step. He himself knew he was no longer the tom he once had been. As if questioning his own ability, he hesitated before the risers of the stairs. Then he might try a jump. Failing, go to a corner to curl up into sleep. "He would look so embarrassed," Evelyn said.

"Confused is the word," Annamary interrupted. "He couldn't understand what was happening to him. Like for most of us, old age came as an unexpected surprise."

They were living in a third floor apartment downtown at this time. Gustaff had the habit of taking his afternoon nap, which began in the morning and lasted until twilight, on the window sill. The window was always open because Gustaff liked it that way. One afternoon he seemed to lose his sense of direction and he rolled right out the open window. He fell three stories into the cement parking area.

There was a great flap. The emergency vet was called. Neighbors barricaded the entrance to the lot to prevent anyone from driving in. The vet very tenderly examined the old cat while a circle of very silent lookers-on held their breaths for him. The conclusion was sad. The vet said nothing was to be done. Gustaff had internal injuries and would probably die during the night. With infinite sadness Annamary and Pauline carried the little speckled body upstairs. They placed him in his usual bed which was on the floor by Annamary. As she went to bed she heard him cry. A good sign as he had been in shock, silent until that moment. Annamary rushed to his bedside and began to comfort and pet him. He lay still. After a time she went back to her bed. Gustaff cried piteously. She rose to attend him and he quieted. Every time she went to bed he reacted and she had to come back to hunker by the catbed. Finally she lifted his sore body and lay it beside the pillow on her own bed so as to offer him solace. Gustaff cried. No. He wanted to be in his own bed but with an attendant. These were his requirements and they were lovingly acceded to. They thought he was surely going to die so they took turns all that night touching him and cooing to him.

Gustaff lived for four more years.

ROSEMARY'S BABIES

I went over to Rosemary's house to help her. She is always planning some benign skullduggery. Rosemary Fingerhat is the president of the Ailurophile Society even though there is no board of directors, no rules, no president not even an Ailurophile Society really. It's all rather imaginary like the equator or the smile on the Cheshire cat, and it is always fun.

As I set about to join her in her manipulations I continually reminded myself of how much was fanciful about our endeavors. There was no cat club, therefore it needed no president. I have to say, however, I've seen Rosemary do wonders with the tenuous authority that the Society afforded her. I've seen that she could mend broken hearts, cure depression and other psychological conditions, and urge action in the faintest of hearts. In addition, she was aggressive in the placing of abandoned or homeless cats ... I believed in her.

Rosemary's house was surprisingly devoid of cat tchatchkis. No pictures of cats. No statuettes. No kitty playing cards. No ashtrays in the form of cats. No flower pots shaped like mama cats with nursing kittens. No cat stuff. But it was a mess. Rosemary had nine children. Three of her grown sons were still living at home. They owned and ran the best car repair shop in the town. At home they were hellions. They trashed the place every day. Although she claimed she had tried to teach them manners, the lesson never took. Rosemary's cat, Mr. Edgar Allen Poe, full of his own dignity, despaired of the mess and usually stationed himself overhead on top of the bookcase, poised like the raven evermore.

Down below the waters roiled. Old hamburger containers, paper cups, plastic utensils rushed together in the infernal sea and attested to a dedicated use of fast food emporia. This was the preferred lifestyle of Rosemary's three sons, Peter, Teddy, and Flip. Burping and farting were their specialties. They reveled in toilet talk and body images. They existed to make each other laugh and to make their mother cringe.

Edgar Allen Poe seemed unperturbed. Nevertheless, we could tell that he quietly hated living in such a porcine nest.

Of course, there were more cats. They belonged to the "boys." Each son claimed a cat. Peter had Stilts (often called "Shits" as if by error), a cat with the longest legs I have ever seen. He was the kind of a cat that gets too excited when offered food. Once I presented him with a delicious treat and he two-stepped so hard that he kept falling over his own long legs and ending up with his face on the floor. The brothers screamed with mirth. The youngest two brothers had two litter mates frivolously named Spit and Achtooey. Everything about the mess, the cats, their mother's frustration, struck the boys as howlingly funny.

"I don't know what to do, Skinny," Rosemary said to me one day. "I'm forever neating things up but it is like sweeping in front of a hurricane. And the body noises are absolutely devastating to me. Nobody needs to be so publicly flatulent! They are more than ten years older than when they left high school, but not an iota more socialized."

"I know the cure for male territorial excesses," I announced. "Rosemary Fingerhat, your boys need to get wives!"

The effect was electric There was a moment of terrible silence. I could have sworn Edgar Allen Poe emitted a mournful syllable in honor of the lost Lenore. Stilts rushed in so fast he tumbled with all four legs tangled. Spit ran in followed by a puffed out Achtooey. Rosemary looked dazed. Then she looked astonished. "Wives!" she gasped. "Of course! Wives. Why didn't I think of that? Skinny Malinck, get your gear together. We have a lot of work to do."

But our work didn't really begin to get underway until Phoebe Pitts, my sweet little neighbor, came by with a new problem. Phoebe frequently appeals to me as sort of a substitute auntie. She ran over to tell me that her car was meowing! She owned an old Volkswagen that was almost defunct but did manage to get her around the block now and then. It was so old that it had no gauges. When Phoebe thought she was low on gas she would stop the old crate and push down a kind of dipstick she kept under the hood to see the gas level. There were undoubtedly smarter ways to do things but Phoebe was a little dopey. Hearing her car meowing had thrown her into absolute confusion. She ran over to my house.

"My car is saying meow!"

"Phoebe, I think you must have a cat under the hood."

"You think so? But I started the car. Do you think I killed it?"

"Is it still meowing?"

"Yes."

I looked at her in wonder. Dopey as she was she was flamingly pretty. She had a pair of huge wondering blue eyes and a curling mane of golden hair. Since when was being kind of dopey a detriment to romance? "Phoebe, I said," we have to extricate this pussycat. And seeing that this car of yours is about as close to a museum piece as one can get, I suggest we call someone really first-rate. My suggestion would be to get one of the Fingerhat boys."

Teddy Fingerhat came out. As he pulled forth from the ancient vehicle a gray striped kitten he said, "Happens all the time with these old hump backed-models. Cats crawl into motors to get warm. Of course, on this car the motor's in the back." He sounded very knowledgeable and in his strong hands he held a frightened kitten. Phoebe's eyelids began to flutter. She gave to Teddy a wide look of blue-eyed admiration. I took a quick glance at Teddy's face and thought I recognized something both ancient and new kindling there.

The minute I got in the house I phoned Rosemary.

"One down, two to go," I said.

She understood what I meant.

MRS. FARKAS

I saw in the paper that Mrs. Farkas was still alive. Her name was listed with major contributors to music programs in the town. Mrs. Farkas was my high school music teacher. At the time, I thought she must be about ninety years old, but that's not possible. Teen agers are always apt to exaggerate adults' ages. Even then Mrs. Farkas was very gray-haired and rather stooped. She gave an aged impression yet she probably was no more than in her in her fifties when she taught at the high school.

Mrs. F. was one of my favorite teachers. Her gentle voice and patient presentation of musical classics to us unruly savages converted us to an appreciation of the finer things. The kids just loved her. She had a dry humor, which endeared her even more. She also had the gift of communicating her enthusiasms. I remembered that she confided in us; she shared with us her romantic dream. She was saving every penny, she said, resolved that on the very day of retirement she and her beloved George, also a musicologist, would embark on a musical

94

tour of the world. She spoke raptures of the various musical festivals. Vienna was her favorite topic. Beautiful Vienna. Romantic Vienna. Mrs. Farkas had posters of the special places on the classroom walls. The great museums of art. The sensuous paintings of Klimt. The dancing white horses. Music everywhere. She almost sang when she spoke of Vienna. Mozart, her favorite, resided there once. His spirit still did.

I thought it would be nice to visit Mrs. Farkas if I could find her. Perhaps it would be a comfort for her in her old age to know she was remembered as fondly as I remembered her. I looked in the directory and there she was, Lucy Farkas. She lived in a nice little residential enclave of the town right around the corner from the Municipal Center. I thought I need make a very short visit of it.

As soon as she came to the door I could see something was strained. She stared so. The entryway was rather dim. "Who are you?" she asked sharply. Maybe she didn't remember me. I felt strange and embarrassed.

"Sally Malinck," I said.

"Skinny? Skinny Malinck who drowned in the sink?" That was the silly rhyme the kids used to taunt me with in the golden days of my youth. But Mrs. Farkas was not teasing. She had opened wide her arms and enfolded me with great affection. She remembered. There were tears in her blue eyes. "You remember the days, Skinny? Bright sun-in-the-afternoon classroom days? The record player that stuttered? Remember the glorious music?"

"I remember." We sat to visit and I looked hard at Mrs. Farkas. Her hair was completely white now. She seemed a little shaky, sort of feeble. I thought she might be ill. I saw her affix a complicated hearing apparatus to her left ear.

Mrs. Farkas began to recall episodes of those bright days of long ago, but she remembered such gloomy things. She remembered some cruel things. She remembered how Nancy Creech had cried when the kids called her Nancy Creature, and voted her Class Freak and posted it on the board. She remembered Greg Long. He died of an overdose when his friends taunted him into using those pills. She remembered the Slam Book which had shamed and criticized half the class.

"It was nothing but teasing," she said. "And teasing is so terrible. Whole schools get shot up over teasing these days."

"But we had good times, too, Mrs. F.," I protested.

"Oh, yes. You were all young. There was promise in the air. There was hope. And dreams."

"Your dream!" I exclaimed. What about your dream? The one you always told us about?"

"The dream ended before it could begin, Skinny. We had tickets for ocean travel when George, my husband and soul mate, died suddenly. It was just two weeks after I retired. My heart died with him. At the same time my hearing was beginning to fail. I grew more and more deaf. I am almost completely deaf now. Not much fun to travel the world alone. Not so much fun to go to concerts now either."

Oh, she felt low. I could see it. "Don't you feel bad though, Skinny," she said. "Sometimes the great symphonies play themselves in my head."

"That's good," I said but I didn't believe it. I felt terribly sad. Mrs. F.'s dream had always been so real to me. As I left I thought it would be fitting to tell her something nice so I said, "You gave me music," because that was true.

But I did keep thinking about her in that small apartment with only the imaginary music and her dreams of George Farkas in heaven, which was a place something like Vienna.

I thought of her often. The next time I saw Rosemary Fingerhat I told her the very sad tale.

"She sounds depressed," Rosemary said.

"Well, yeah."

"I know the cure."

"What?"

"The cure for depression."

"And what would that be, Smartypants?"

"A kitten. No one can be depressed with a kitten in the house."

"Oh, come on, Ro. I would never dream of giving someone a living kitten. It's an expense and a responsibility."

"Of course, that's right. You must never give anyone a living animal unless it's wanted and going to a welcoming home."

"Mrs F. is a kind lady all right. She saved me from many a tight spot when I was a high school cut-up. But I still wouldn't park a cat on her."

"A kitten. Kittens are special. They mend broken hearts."

"Still -- no."

"You haven't heard my plan."

"Okay. Spill it."

This was Rosemary's plan – to appear at Mrs. F's door with a kitten safely encased in a carrier. On the excuse that I had business at the Municipal Center I would ask permission to leave the cat in Mrs. F's apartment for an hour or two. If there was the least sign of softness in the response, I would ask if it would be all right to let the kitten run free. "I'm telling you, Skinny, I am going to provide a magic kitty. Guaranteed to induce happiness."

"And if she doesn't want it?" I countered.

"This will be a magic kitten. She will want it."

I let her talk me into it and, soon after, embarked on this mission with a really beautiful kitten provided by Rosemary Fingerhat. He was a Russian blue with fur that actually looked silver. His nose and the pads of his feet were the same silver color. He truly was a beautiful little animal.

Mrs. Farkas was very surprised at my request, but melted at the sight of the kitten. "What a pretty baby!" she said.

"It's really kind of you to let me leave him here, Mrs. F. I'll only be an hour or two. I will return to collect him as soon as I finish my errand. I just can't lug a cat into those offices over there."

"That's quite all right." The kitten was climbing on the carrier wall to get out. "It doesn't like the cage though, Skinny. Would it be okay if I let him out?" she said.

I knew then. She was hooked.

When I returned she was smiling in the old way, a twinkle in her blue eyes. "I've had fun with the kitten," she declared. "I played with him for an hour. He was so happy to run and jump after a piece of string. Then he climbed up on to my lap and went to sleep. So soft. So soft! And, you know what, I could hear him! Well, not hear him exactly. With my hand over his little body I could tell he was purring."

"Thank you so much for cat sitting for me, Mrs. Farcas. Now I'll take him to the shelter. He's a little orphan. I have to find a permanent home for him."

Well, I don't need to tell you what happened next. Just as Rosemary had told me, it was a magic kitten.

MOTHER LOVE

Tillie Kukla had cause to doubt the evidence of her eyes. At eighty seven she knew her visual acuity was less than it should be. Often she was accused of seeing things that were not there or not seeing things that actually were. Lately she had noticed, or thought she had noticed a dark shape stealthily creeping through the tall grass of her yard. The dark shadow seemed headed for the back of her chicken coop. She much feared a skunk or a badger had decided to dine on the fresh food back there. The usual burglar alarm was the dogs' uproar or the immediate cackling of seventeen articulate hens, but that had not yet happened. She dared not investigate in the night as critters with teeth were not unknown in the area. The next morning, she ventured out to see about the disturbance.

She discovered a lump of kittens. She counted three of them, all rolled up together in a warm furry ball.

But she had only time to make a quick count when a fury descended from the top of the coop. An angry demon, all fangs and deadly claws, was threatening her with its violent maternity. Tillie retreated very carefully, circumspect and respectful. She saw that her dogs, too, stayed a careful distance away as, wanting to defend her, they lacked the courage to face this spitting fiend.

The next day she ventured out that way. The nest was gone with all its kits and, while she wondered about that, she noted some activity at the other shed. She approached to find the door slightly open. She opened it wide. Again, the wrath of the mother was awakened.

She did not look for the little family again. She was aware that they lived with their highly wrathful dam somewhere on the property and she gave them their berth.

One morning about three weeks later, Tillie went to her front door and the three kittens had been carefully placed there. That wild Mother, called away for some feline business, had found this way to provide for the future of her precious children.

Tillie took it for the honor it was.

SWEET WILLIAM

John said the cats went everywhere they weren't wanted. They were undisciplined and insolent. Every time he would chase one off the counter another would appear, smiling at him. Yes, smiling! He felt he was overrun by Cheshire cats; Cheshire cats just like in the storybook, and they were always giving him those smartass smiles. John knew they must be saying, "In your face! Ha ha!" In addition to the cats there were three hyperactive shihtzu dogs. They were not so many, but they were frenetic. They chased everything that moved and John could almost hear them yelling, "Whoopee!" every second leap, oblivious to his precarious nervous system.

Despite the constant cries of SCAT! and expletives reminding the dogs that they really were the embodiment of the first syllable of their breed's name, John loved all the animals.

"Shihtzu! You little shit!" rang out over a favorite shoe that was chomped to a soggy glob. But that was as far as he went discipline-wise.

He couldn't help laughing when he scolded them. He thought it was funny when he demanded, "Who did this?" and all three dogs looked guilty.

The animals fared very well with John. The shihtzus loved the cats and kissed them at every opportunity. The cats, with magnificent disdain, managed to ignore the dogs' wet adoration. Everyone got fed and watered and petted regularly. There was continuous confusion but it was benign. Though John was a little overrun, he was not a hoarder. He just had a big house and a big heart to go with it. Any vagrant, any stray could find sanctuary at John's.

One day as he drove up his drive he noticed a large coyote. It loped away as soon as it saw the car. John came out of his car to the sounds of distress. Up in the tallest tree was a very small kitten setting up a general alarm. To no avail, John made coaxing noises, Finally he went to the shed and got the long ladder to rescue the frightened animal.

The cat had a collar, far too tight on his little neck, but no indications of ownership. And he was terribly scrawny. John got some smelly cat food and the kitten went into raptures. Thus Sweet William was adopted into the family.

He was a major pest. He was the pestiest of the menagerie. He jumped into every open space. He teased the dogs. He raced up the curtains and scratched on the furniture. He soaked the living room rug trying to catch fish out of the aquarium. When he was hungry he set up a god-awful clamor until not just food but delectable food was offered. In short, Sweet William was a very irresistible cat.

And he was a baby. That was obvious in his size and behavior. When John heard him crying an alarm one afternoon he feared that the large coyote had returned a repeat engagement. He ran outside to intervene. Sweet William was on the roof. How he got up there was a mystery. He didn't seem to know how to get down. John called and called. Panic prevailed. The cat kept screaming. He wouldn't even attempt the jump.

Again, John went to the shed to get the long ladder. Reluctantly he ascended to the roof. Catching Sweet William was another story as the cat was spooked and did not cooperate. John got out on the roof.

A determined Arizona wind was blowing. The ladder fell over. John and Sweet William were on the roof. John pondered what to do. He stood and made himself as large as he could. Cars were passing along the road in front of the house but they flew right by. They either did not see him or did not realize his dilemma.

The sun was going down. John was beginning to get cold when his neighbor, returning from work, noticed he was on the roof and came to rescue him. As he came down the ladder he realized Sweet William was no where to be seen.

Not on the roof, anyway. No, he was sitting on the ground watching John descend.

On his face was that insolent smile.

GARRULOUS CAT

A cat came to my friend Dolly Mudd's kitchen window sill almost every morning. Dolly told me all about her. The cat was not a stray. She wore an expensive collar bedizened with sparkles, so it was clear that somebody loved her. She came as a visitor. She wanted to chat with Dolly and Dolly appreciated the visit. Since the jeweled collar gave no indication of name or owner my friend decided to call the visitor Lucille after her favorite comedienne. This Lucille was also red headed, and with a droll white face. She knew how to be funny, too.

There was no doubt that Lucille had a reason for coming to Dolly's house. She came to talk. On the mornings when Doll became aware of Lucille's presence on the window sill she'd open the window in welcome. Sometimes Lucille came in and sometimes not. She was a graceful guest. She could pussy foot her way down over the faucets and the dish rack and the sink without disturbing anything.

Dolly was familiar with the exercise. She was to go sit in the big easy chair. Lucille would follow her and position herself on the small nearby table. Now, as their heads were on a plane, she was in her favorite position for conversation. After a few minutes she would give out a short series of meows. Then it was Dolly's turn to say something.

"Really?" Doll might reply, stressing the question mark.

Now Lucille would develop the discursive details. Some fraught meows explained the situation.

"Well, that's amazing," Dolly would remark, or something of that ilk.

Occasionally Dolly would emit a gentle series of chuckles. If Lucille nodded, Doll knew it was the right response. And the cat, nodding her rusty head, would utter a few mellow meows. The mood was pleasant and conversational. Typically the colloquy lasted from ten to fifteen minutes. Then Lucille would leap up to the window sill and depart, but not before delivering the final meow which Doll assumed was a polite goodbye.

But there were times when Lucille did not jump down into the room for a real chat. She paused on the windowsill and delivered herself of a sharp series of squawks. Dolly then knew she was being told about something disagreeable that happened at home. Remarks like "Oh, that's too bad" or "I'm so sorry" passed but such remarks were cut off. Lucille always had to have the last meow.

When I last visited. Dolly pointed out Lucille to me. The cat was walking in the garden. Every now and then she would stop and nod her head.

"What do you think ails her, Dolly?"

"Nothing," Doll replied. "She's just talking to herself."

CAT SCRAMBLE

THE CUSP

Peony Flowers is one of the sweetest people I know, one of the prettiest as well. She is known for her humor and unflagging spirit. Indeed, to know her is to love her. The Ailurophile Society came to both know and love her on the occasion of the demise of her comical cat, Napoleon. Napoleon was a cat with a sense of humor, a suitable cat for Peony who is jocular and always sees the funny side. Napoleon's specialty was hiding behind low furniture and then leaping out as if to mount a mock attack on passing legs. After each attack he would withdraw. It was so clearly a game that everyone had to forgive him even if it meant some depredations on innocent socks and stockings. He was so funny. He played peek-a-boo and chase-me with the best. Napoleon was a constant source of delight and then one day -- POOF! He was gone, it was believed the victim of some ailurophobe poisoner. Peony mourned but only for a little while. It was at this sad juncture of her life that

Peony joined the Ailurophile Society and set about establishing the Napoleon No-Kill shelter on the east side of town.

Being attractive and of a generous spirit, Peony had in no time attracted some consolers of the opposite sex. Foremost amongst these was Catullus Pugh, one of the town aldermen. Cattulus Pugh was a grouch, a self-important, cantankerous curmudgeon. No one could stand him but Peony Flowers. She liked him – a lot. When asked for an explanation she replied, "It's a mutual thing. That's all I can say. And don't you love his name, Skinny?" she asked me. "Catullus. It's classical Roman and feline at the same time."

"Hmmm. The short form would be Cat, I suppose."

"Right, but he might not like that. He's very formal, you know. "

"I've noticed."

"I have always hated my own silly name," Peony declared.

"Oh, yes. Peony. I can imagine what they did to that in grade school."

"I don't mean Peony. I mean my last name."

"Peony, if you marry Catullus you have to consider your name will become Peony Pugh!" I commented.

"Ugh" she said but she almost laughed her head off over that.

And she married him anyhow.

The man was such a stuffed shirt and phony that we all worried about that union. Peony seemed delighted with his pomposity. She found every excuse to poke pins in his balloon. And Catullus seemed delighted to be poked. He was actually learning to laugh at himself. I guess he loved her.

"Skinny, I just have to tell you the latest. You know, soon after we moved into our new house, I acquired a cat. Marie Antoinette is her name and she is a sweetie, a real lady. She is so fastidious that she not only flushes her toilet but, after eating, she always washes her dishes.

"Every morning it's Catullus' habit to settle into the bathroom for a long session of reading the paper and attending to the necessities. Apparently, it's quite a big production. Some mornings he's in there almost an hour. The morning after we moved into the new house I heard Catullus screaming in the bathroom. I ran in to see the problem and there was my lord and master, his pants down on the floor, and Marie Antoinette happily ensconced in the crotch of Catullus Pugh's downcast trousers!

ELVIS

"Some say that men hate cats," said Jeffrey Viramontes, the Dean at the Community College. He had just joined a gathering of ailurophiles when I was having my cappuccino in Joe's JavaNutt. "As far as I'm concerned, it's a base canard. I have always admired cats for their beauty, their dignity, and their independent spirit.

"When I was a boy I lived in a cottage by Lake Wakapo. My brother Kevin and I spent the most wonderful years there. We were free as the breezes and surrounded by wild nature, a perfect life for young boys. We swam, we fished. We built elaborate tree houses that usually collapsed. We even hunted in spite of a father who hated blood sports. Not much blood was spilled in our predatory adventures, however. We hunted with nets and ropes. It was an exercise in patience. We would set up our lucky sites and our complex rope traps, then hide and lie still in the high grass in the hope that something would be stupid enough to walk right in. Then, at least in theory, POOM! pop our little nets over the victim's head. I think Dad supplied us with butterfly nets for this enterprise. He was very averse to hunting in all forms but he acceded to our boyish dreams. As he anticipated, with our sad equipment we never caught anything except occasional butterflies. For an interminable list of ecological reasons which Dad would enumerate at length, we always had to let the butterflies and bugs go.

"One day a big cat jumped into one of our rope traps. This is the way we visualized it: Some small animal had become entangled in the ropes. Even if we had never succeeded in catching anything in our traps we believed that. We thought this funny looking cat had pounced down on our quarry. The mouse or vole or whatever had escaped and the cat had gotten entangled. Not very plausible but there it was. A really funny looking feline was sitting on our complicated but mostly useless trap.

"Now this world shaking event happened on January eighth of a year I can no longer remember though I will always remember the date. Does it not mean anything to you? Jeffrey said.

I admit I was mystified.

" No? Then you are to be pitied, if you will excuse me saying so.

"The birthday of the King, himself!

"We immediately named the cat Elvis.

"Elvis appeared to be a stray. Aside from being mortally dirty he had only one ear and he had a crimp in his tail that bent it on a 180 degree angle right near his body. He still managed to wave this cockeyed tail majestically. Under the dirt he was a very common sort of black and white cat, but he had a white chin and marked white sideburns. Beneath his pink nose was a crooked line of white which prompted Kevin to call him Fu Man Chu at times and El Zorro at others. He had a lot of aliases as befits an outlaw, and outlaw he was. He leapt on the counter to check the dinner. If he approved he quickly snatched his share. He jumped up on the mantelpiece and knocked down all the precious pictures of our mother. Worst of all, when Dad was writing his long and very important dissertation, Elvis would get up on the desk and swat at Dad's pencil. Angrily Dad would cry out, 'Elvis! No!' Dad would swat back at the boy. Elvis would scoot. Of course, Elvis believed it all to be a great game. Kevin and I would be doubling over with laughter."

"Was he a singing cat?" I asked.

"I expected that question. And yes, Elvis could sing. Every once in a while he would raise his voice in a commanding song. Dad usually said, 'He needs to go out now.' We didn't ask why. Elvis trotted out into the woods and sometimes he was gone for days. Kevin and I mourned him. We missed the scurvy bum.

"We thought he must be lost or eaten by hawks but he always returned, exhausted and very much the worse for wear but, I think, happy.

"When the warm weather came Dad brought out a dilapidated old row boat that was in the shed. This he worked over carefully, applying many coats of caulking. Then with admonitions for our safe and responsible behavior he let us at it.

"A pirate life on the open sea is what we envisioned. No sooner had we arranged ourselves in the boat than Elvis jumped in. He took a commanding position in the stern and sat there waiting for us to set sail.

"As I recall there was some brotherly grappling going on over the oars. Some confusion. The next thing we knew Elvis was in the water. We thought he'd drown but instead he swam. His crooked tail furled out like a dark water snake. He swam to the shore. Kevin blamed me but I thought it was Kevin's fault. 'You almost killed our cat!'

"Had we knocked Elvis over? Apparently not because the next time we got out the rowboat Elvis came and sat himself regally in the stern.

"This time we were careful and saw what he did. A little way off from land he jumped right into the water. It was a conscious choice. Again he swam to shore. From then on any time we got the boat out Elvis came to participate in the outing. We never could get him to enter the water from the shore. He liked to start from deeper water.

"Elvis stayed with us for a few years but one day he set out for an amorous adventure from which he never returned. We were sad.

"My brother now owns a cattery in Florida and raises prize Abyssinians. Beautiful cats but he admits that there never has been such a cat as Elvis.

"He was a star."

JOSE/JOSEFINA

Roberta Hogg told me this tale of identity crisis. Not long after they were married, newlyweds Walter and Patty Beasley moved into the apartment upstairs from her. They had no idea of what was to be done or how to do it. They were so cute and dopey. Patty frequently slipped downstairs to get Roberta's expert opinion on matters of cookery, housecleaning, faucet drips and dealing with the inevitable maintenance men.

Patty was blonde and pigtailed and dressed in shorts in all weathers, Roberta thought she looked no more than twelve years old. Walter had his first job on the entry level of management in the big new Mountainmart. He had to wear a suit and tie to work and it was, perhaps, the first time in his life he had to thus bedeck himself and pretend to be a grown man. As far as Roberta was concerned, however, he looked like a little boy in a Halloween costume. The clothes perhaps even more than his new and responsible semi-executive position made him a little self-important, but on the whole he was sweet. Roberta grew quite fond of them. The kids were in a very romantic phase of life and Roberta couldn't help smiling when she thought of the love nest upstairs. Of course, she was certainly not a meddler. On the matter of first love she just tended to wax somewhat sappy.

With his first pay check Walter decided a celebration was in order. They drove the long way into Serrano where Walter had heard there was an outstanding restaurant called Jose's. Before the fifty mile journey Patty had several times descended to check withRoberta on the proper dress. You'd think Jose's was a night club in Paris. At their stage of life everything was a first, an adventure. Roberta knew Jose's was a mediocre place but had no doubt the kids' naiveté and excitement would imbue it with all the necessary romantic overtones.

The next morning she heard Patty calling her from the stairwell. Roberta was eager to hear about the grand celebration. "Roberta! Roberta! Can you come up? I have something to show you!" There was a note of urgency in the invitation and Roberta obeyed.

The apartment was just like her own but very sparsely furnished. They were newlyweds after all, just making a start.

"Here, Roberta. "Over here!" Patty cried. She led her over to the armchair, the only chair in the room. Lying supine upon it, as if with every legal right, was a small grey cat. "We found him wandering around Jose's last night." Patty declared. "He's obviously without a home. Walt said we could keep him." Patty eyes sparkled as she picked up the young animal and carried it over for Roberta's inspection. "He said we could keep him if he was a boy. We didn't want to have any mess with kittens. So Walt looked and, sure enough, he's a boy!" Well, Roberta didn't know. She's a respectable maiden lady that doesn't know much about anything of that sort. Gently she tried to explain benefits of spaying and neutering, regardless of sex. Patty just laughed. She was having none of it "Well we can't pay for anything like that now but, if he's a boy, he will at least never come home, pregnant will he?"

"I guess not," Roberta said, but she was not happy about it.

"We're going to call him Jose after the restaurant!"

Time passed and Jose grew. Walter complained that he was never allowed to sit in the armchair any more. Jose had taken over. If Walter sat, he crawled in behind and nudged. Walt might have resented it if he had not thought it was funny. Jose was beginning to be a man-about-town and ranged the neighborhood, making friends and looking for handouts. "He's free-loading around the area. Look how fat he's getting." Patty said.

Roberta sighed meekly, "Yes, I see," she said.

Before long Jose began to meowl around more than usual. His call had an unusual ring to it. As days passed the cry began to sound absolutely imperative. At about this time I arrived on the scene, visiting my friend Roberta Hogg. I looked into the front yard and saw Jose yelling his head off in the middle of a small band of disreputable looking tomcats. Patty was coming down the stairs. "Patty, who told you this cat was a male?" I asked.

"Walter," Patty said. Then there was a loaded pause while gears shifted in Patty's head. "Roberta, do you think my cat is a girl?"

"What do you think, Skinny?"

"I do think you've got a girl here, honey, and I think she's about ready to pop."

"Oh-my-god, oh-my-god!" Patty squealed. She was hyperventilating and beginning to go into a panic. "I don't know what to do. Please come up with me."

"Don't worry. The cat knows what to do," I assured her ... but apparently he did not. As long as we both stood by the birthing box Jose was quiet but if we moved away he set up a terrible squall. It really was not fair. He'd been told he was a boy for all those long months. How could he have expected such a shocking reversal?

In short order Jose gave birth to three pretty kits and settled back into her new life as Josefina with only a minimum of the psychological scars such a switch might involve.

DOGS ARE PEOPLE TOO

This was the cat story Isabelle Gooch told me. "Many years ago when we first had installed the outdoor pool we kids sat in the kitchen admiring the blueness of it. One day something bright yellow flashed over the garden wall and landed in the center of the pool. Whatever it was, it was alive and struggling. Then, as we watched, we saw Bruno, the family dog, leap off the side and swim up to the disturbance. He seemed to go under for a minute and then came up again, right under the yellow splotch. He swam toward the house and splashed his way into the kitchen with the yellow burden on his head.

"The astonishment abated and we examined the yellow mass. It was a very stressed-out golden kitten. As soon as Bruno had shaken out about a gallon of pool water he was carrying around, he sat down beside the kitten and the kitten climbed back up on his head. Bruno lay down for a much deserved nap and the kitty, likewise, zonked out for a nap. When somewhat later we had the chance to examine him we found the kitten to be about two months old, a male of an indiscriminate breed, a bright shade, almost chrome yellow. His tail was faintly striped but there was not much else remarkable about him except that he was as yellow as sunshine, rode around on a dog's head, and had arrived by air express. We called him Hattie.

"Could he fly? All of us had seen Hattie come hurtling over the pool. Could he have jumped from the top of the wall?

"Mama arrived to check out the excitement in the yard. She was a little overwhelmed by the new addition to the family. By Mama's proclamation Hattie was adopted and, by virtue of his special adaptations, remained for many years a lid to adorn Bruno's head. The dog continued to wear Hattie proudly and Hattie loved the dog.

"'But Mama,'" said Jerry, who was only four years old at that time, 'This kitty can fly! I saw it!'

"She didn't argue but we older children knew that there were bad people in the world. We lived in a neighborhood of big houses with high stone walls and, sometimes lousy people threw over things they didn't want.

"But we did want Hattie and he wanted us. He stayed with us, often transported by Bruno.

"Eventually Bruno died in the culmination of his many good years. Hattie became disconsolate. He sniffed the old corners, the well-worn rugs. Nothing would suit until one day Papa brought home a little puppy. Its head was too small for Hattie, but Hattie settled into warm companionship and his tale was told and retold endlessly around the family hearth."

MRS. FARKAS REVISITED

When on a cold morning Snowflake decided to sleep beside me under the warm comforter I thought loving thoughts. He is so tiny that I was at first afraid I'd crush him in one of my nocturnal twisting, but there was no need to fear. He was amazingly agile. He scooted away into a new position even as I thought of turning. He was, of course, endowed with sixth and seventh and possibly even with eighth senses, senses that are peculiar to a midget deaf kitty. To think that this was the tiny being rescued from the dross by that wonderful witch, Imelda Pogue.

And Dr. Woo. And me. Of course, me. I was part of the rescue team.

Feeling omnipotent, I thought of all the good works I had assumed under the influence of Rosemary Fingerhat and the Ailurophile Sociiety. With gentle kindness and treats galore we had taught Rodney Bloomer's Egyptian Mau not to spit and thereby reconciled Louise to both the cat and the Ailurophile Society. I had been civil to DOCTOR Alda

Patalda and even managed to find her a few five dollar customers for her outré theories of cat language. As a matter of fact, the introduction to Xantippe Glotz had resulted in a fast friendship between the two loony women, a true union of the crazies.

Olivia Pitts and Teddy Fingerhat were, by now, so beautifully in love that he responded no more to vulgarity or gutter humor, only to poetry and flowers.

Homes would have been found for all three of Angela Paloo's kittens except that she and her dogs became so fond of them that she decided to keep them.

The wandering minstrel, now known as Pavarotti lived in Apache Heights in harmony with all, especially Mona Lisa Buggmeister. The English bulldog.

I congratulated myself. I wondered about the many cats who were not rescued from garbage cans, remained entangled in spaghetti strands or banana peels, were never rescued to live the blessed life to which they were entitled by their very feline fortunes. I called Rosemary Fingerhat to brag a little. She had been partner or instigator of so many of my adventures that I felt like hearing her melodious voice.

"Right, Skinny. We did good. What about your depressed friend?"

"Who?"

"You know. Your old school teacher. The one we gave the Russian blue to?"

"Oh, right! Mrs. Farcas. I think it's time I visit her again."

"Another merciful errand? I'll come along." Rosemary said.

Delighted to have her, I rang Mrs. F who declared herself equally delighted to have both of us. And the kitten, now a plump silver adolescent was clearly delighted with everyone and romped and played and begged us for loving attention. Mrs. Farcas looked proud and pleased. "What do you think of Wolfgang? He is the prettiest, lovingest kitty. I adore him! You know, Skinny, if my hand is on his body, which it often is, I can *hear* him purr and meow and guess his very thoughts."

Clearly the cure for depression had worked.

"And I love his color," Mrs. F. continued. "He's a consistent and magnificent silver from his nose to the soles of his paddy paws. He is so beautiful."

"And so your life goes better, Mrs. F?"

"Indeed. Joy follows joy. I have had marvelous contacts with several musical societies that are going to publish some of George Farcas' musical writings. George would have been so proud and I am so proud to have brought forth his papers.

"And look at this!" She handed us a framed photo of two beautiful girls. "These are George's nieces, Dodo and Cookie Farcas."

"They are perfect counterparts of each other," Rosemary remarked. "One so blond and one so dark," said Rosemary Fingerhat.

"Yes, they're twins. Nineteen years old this spring."

"Both beauties," I remarked.

"The really wonderful part," Said Mrs. Farcas "is that they are coming here! Tonight!" She beamed at us. "They are enrolled in the college and will stay at the dormitory. I am just sorry that the Welcome Dance for new students is tomorrow night. They do not yet know anyone, so will not be able to go to the dance."

"Girls like these never have trouble finding escorts," said Rosemary.

I gave her a sharp look. "We know some nice young men who would be most happy to squire them to the dance," I said. I actually poked my elbow into Rosemary's side.

Rosemary jumped. She finally got it. "Yes! I will command two princes to be ready to escort these princesses tomorrow night," she laughed.

Sitting by the framed photo, magnificent in silver, Wolfgang Amadeus Mozart emitted two sharp musical notes to indicate his satisfaction with the proceedings.

Rosemary and I exchanged beatific smiles. The rest we knew we could safely leave to Nature.

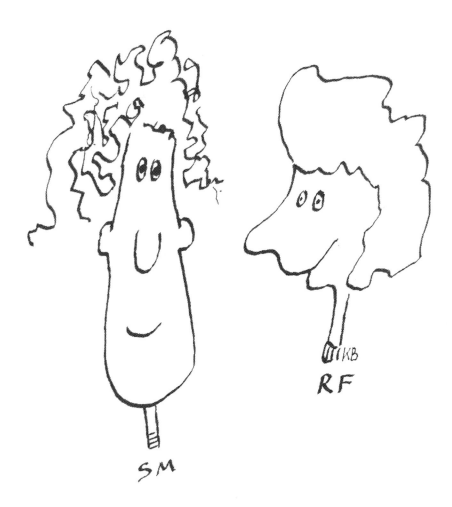